IF I COULD REWIND THE TIME

MUFADDAL BAYADWALA

Made with ♥ on the Notion Press Platform
www.notionpress.com

I want to dedicate this book to my parents - Farida and Aliasgar Bayadwala, my brother and sister-in-law - Taher and Fatema, and the three loves of my life - wife Nisreen and sons Burhanuddin & Yusuf.

Contents

Foreword

This book is a perfect story for someone who loves the concept of time traveling or wants to rewind his own time. Through this story, the benefits and drawbacks are perfectly explained regarding the time rewind.

Preface

Most of the time, people think that if they could rewind their time and go back to their past to live those happy days again, or to avoid certain mistakes so that they could improve their lives, or again live with someone who is no more. I am one of them. But we all know that time rewind is not possible.

Still, I wanted to experience what it feels like to go to the past. I used to imagine how a person would feel if he or she got a chance to rewind the time. So, an idea clicked in my mind. The idea was to develop a story of a guy, who gets a chance to rewind his time. So, I happened to write this book.

Acknowledgements

For this book, my first thanks go to my mom Farida, and dad Aliasgar who always trusted me for this. They were the first to see the writer inside me and encourage me to write. Then, my biggest thanks go to my wonderful wife Nisreen. She was the one to hold my hand when I had almost given up on writing.

My brother Taher and sister-in-law Fatema have also guided me up to a huge level so that I can be a successful writer. Thank you very much both of you.

But there is one more thing. The biggest reason why I am a successful author is my friend's group - MAGIC. It was December 2011, when all my childhood friends - Darshan Kabra, Alfiya Saifee, Minal Mehta, Dinesh Jain, Raunak Laddha, Nikita Tiwari, Taher Bayadwala, Sneha Mutha, and Akshat Agrawal had gathered for the new-year party. But as the celebration days were done, all had started moving towards their job towns. I was deeply hurt by getting separated from them. So, I decided to write a poem about them. It was my first poem and everyone loved it a lot. This is how the writer inside me was born. Thank you - Magic Group. I will always owe my success to you.

Prologue

'Tik – tik'. The morning alarm rang. Akash was awakened but was still sleepy. He groped his hand towards the clock on his bedside table to put off the alarm while his head was still under the pillow.

"Akash, wake up." Akash's mother called from downstairs. "It's seven o'clock. Now as your S.S.C. exams are over, that does not mean you are supposed to lie down the whole day."

Akash moved the pillow from his face, rubbed the sleep from his eyes, and sat on his bed. He saw his table clock showing seven o'clock. It was a warm summer morning. The cooler was switched off. He knew it was done by his younger brother Tejas who was off to school as his seventh standard exams were still going on. Only the ceiling fan was on. The morning sunlight entering from his window had filled his room. He stood up and moved towards the wall calendar which showed the date – 20th March 2006, the first day of his three-month holiday. He had ample time with him but he could not realize what he could do with it. He had never thought about his future in earnest.

"Akash, are you coming to have your breakfast or not?" His mother called.

"Yes maa," Akash replied.

While brushing his teeth and having his shower, he was wondering about his passiveness about his life. He wiped himself, got ready in his bedroom, and went down for breakfast.

As he reached downstairs, his parents were shocked to see him in a formal plain shirt and trousers with oily flattened combed hair. Even his father was wearing formal clothes, but he was a businessman and was going to his shop after breakfast. "Where are you going?" His father asked.

"Nowhere," Akash answered.

"So why are you wearing this at home?" His mother asked.

"These are my daily clothes," Akash answered to her. So, his father rested his arms on the dining table and took a deep breath. "Listen, son, you need to upgrade yourself. You have to stop being passive and start learning from your surroundings." As his father was explaining to him, his mother interjected. "Prashant! Please."

"Pratima, let me talk to him," Prashant said calmly. "Look at your classmates' way of living, the way they dress and talk to others. They have already started making decisions regarding their career. Have you decided anything regarding your career?"

"No," Akash said with a blank face. His mother was staring at him.

"Then decide fast." Prashant persuaded Akash. He moved his chair towards him, held his hands, and said, "Son, I don't want to compare you with anyone. I just want you to develop yourself. You can even develop your career from your hobbies and skills. Just ask yourself about the things you are good at." Prashant placed his hand on Akash's head to support him. Then, he stood up and left the room. Akash got a bit nervous. So, Pratima neared him, kissed his forehead, and said, "Don't worry son, everything will be fine. Now have your breakfast." She passed the breakfast plate towards him. He saw that the plate had two freshly cooked chapattis. He applied butter and jam to it, rolled it, and started eating.

Prashant and Pratima had a middle-class family with a simple lifestyle. They did not aim much in life but just wanted their sons to live a life that was different from theirs.

Afterward, Akash went out to call his colony friends to play. Dhaval, Minakshi, Ankita, Dhruv, Nitya, Manish, Sejal, and Rohan were his colony friends. While playing badminton, Nitya asked everyone, "What are you all planning regarding your career?"

"I am taking admission in commerce," Dhaval said while hitting the shuttle cork towards Sejal.

"What are you planning?" Manish asked Nitya.

"I will be doing B.D.S." Nitya replied. "What about you all?"

"I am going for science. After that, I will be doing engineering." Dhruv said.

"Me too," Rohan said.

"Even me," Manish added. Akash was staring at them. He was wordless.

"What kind of hobbies you all are having?" Akash asked.

"I just like watching movies," Ankita said bluntly.

"My hobby is to sleep or play the whole day," Dhaval said. "But why are you asking this?"

"Can we make a career out of our hobbies?" Akash asked.

"Yes of course. Dhaval's hobby is to sleep the whole day. He can play a good role of Kumbhkaran in Ramayan shows." Ankita japed and so everyone had a guffaw.

"Very funny," Dhaval said arrogantly.

"I don't think career and hobbies depend on each other," Sejal said in her soft voice. Everyone turned towards her to listen. "I mean, a career is something by which you can please others like your family, your boss, or your clients and customers. But hobbies are something which you do for yourself."

"It's not necessary. What if someone's hobby is singing? He or she can make a good career out of it." Ankita said.

"By the way Akash, what are your hobbies?" Minakshi asked.

"I don't know," Akash said with embarrassment. "I have still not figured out what I am good at."

The summer afternoon was making them sweat. "It's getting too hot. Let's meet in the evening." Nitya said and so, everyone moved towards their home.

As Akash reached home, he lay on the sofa and switched on the television when his younger brother Tejas was back home from school.

"How was your exam?" Pratima asked while arranging the plates on the dining table.

"It was excellent, maa," Tejas replied happily as he tossed his bag on the sofa. Akash knew his brother Tejas was talented compared to him, though he was three years younger than him. He was not surprised to know that his brother's exam was excellent.

"The lunch is ready. Both of you get fresh and come fast." Pratima called.

Akash, Tejas, and Pratima were having lunch when Tejas said, "Maa, after my tuition classes, my friends will be coming over here for studies. We have got some previous years' question papers to solve."

"That's nice," Pratima said while pouring some rice onto his plate.

"Maa, will you please check our answer sheets?" Tejas asked while having his bite.

"But why don't you do it by yourself?" Pratima asked.

"We don't want to waste time on that," Tejas said.

"But you should check your sheets yourself. By this, you will get to know what mistakes you have made." Pratima said while Akash was just staring at them. He had never wondered why someone would do so much preparation for exams. Pratima caught his eyes, but he immediately looked down at his plate and started eating. She understood what was going on in his mind.

"How many exams are left of yours?" Akash asked Tejas.

"Still four are remaining. Tomorrow I have a science paper." Tejas said. "Now I am leaving."

"All the best." Pratima wished as he left. Even Akash finished his food and went upstairs to his bedroom. While lying on the bed, he was wondering why was he so aimless. He looked at the sky from his window, expecting some guidance from the almighty before he went to sleep.

In the evening, Tejas was back home along with his friends. Akash woke up because of the disturbance they had created while entering the room. They were Atul, Krishna, Ragini, Chetan, Neha, and Akshay. They sat on the floor and distributed copies of the previous years' question papers.

"We will do one thing. We will revise for a couple of hours and then solve these papers individually. Let's see who finishes first and scores the highest." Ragini said and so everyone started their work. Akash was amazed to see their dedication. He left the room out of chagrin and went down to the hall to watch his favorite television show, showing the story of the king of Delhi – Prithviraj Chauhan. He liked historical shows very much and loved to spend his time on them. Afterward, as the show was over, he went out to join his colony friends.

It was eight o'clock in the evening when Prashant returned home from his shop. "Where are the children?" He asked Pratima.

"Tejas is along with his friends in his bedroom, preparing for tomorrow and Akash is with his friends outside," Pratima said.

"Did he decide anything?" Prashant asked.

"Prashant, he needs some time," Pratima said abruptly.

"Pratima, he has only three months to decide which field he likes before his college starts," Prashant said calmly. "Okay, call him. I need to talk to him."

"Prashant please," Pratima said. She was getting uneasy.

"It's not regarding his studies. Just call him." Prashant said. So Pratima went out to bring Akash with her.

"Did you call me, papa?" Akash asked as soon as he entered the house.

"Yes, I called you. Sit." Prashant said and so, Akash sat near him. He was a bit uncomfortable. He thought his father would ask him about his future plans.

"What happened?" He asked nervously.

"Will you join M.S.-C.I.T. classes?" Prashant asked.

"What is M.S.-C.I.T.?" Akash asked.

"It's full is – Maharashtra state certificate in information technology. It's a computer course, starting from coming Monday. The timing is in the morning from eight to ten." Prashant said.

"Okay, I will do it," Akash said randomly.

"Don't say 'yes' impulsively just because I am saying. Are you really interested in the course? Think twice and then decide. Tomorrow is Friday. I will complete the formalities over there and this is the address." Prashant said while passing the visiting card to Akash. It read – Bhansali classes, Plot no 9, Sharda complex, 1st floor, Laxmi road, Jaynagar, Dhran.

"One more thing I want to talk about," Prashant said after taking a gasp. "Have you decided anything regarding your career?"

"Prashant, again you are asking the same thing." Pratima said defiantly but Prashant interjected forcefully, "I know what I am asking. I am not pressurizing him but helping him to make a decision." Pratima was at a loss of words. She could just stare with a glower. Even Tejas had reached down along with his friends. They had heard their talks a bit. "What happened?" Tejas asked. Prashant turned towards him.

"Did you all finish your studies?" Prashant asked Tejas and his friends with a smile.

"Yes, uncle." Tejas' friends replied.

"All the best for tomorrow." Prashant wished them.

"Thank you, uncle." Tejas' friends said and went out. Then, Prashant turned back to Akash and asked, "Will you be able to do architecture?"

"Architecture! Does it mean making buildings?" Akash asked bluntly.

"No, it does not mean constructing buildings, but making the structural drawings of it," Prashant said. Akash gave a bemused look to his parents. He didn't know anything about architecture. But still, he agreed without giving a thought, "Yes papa. I will do it."

CHAPTER ONE

TWO YEARS LATER

It's been two years since Akash decided to go for architecture. Prashant had struggled a lot to get admitted to some good junior colleges because of his low percentage in S.S.C. exams. Now he had finished his H.S.C. exams, but the fear was the same.

It was six o'clock in the morning. The doorbell rang 'Ting-Tong'. Pratima woke up from her sleep immediately and went down to open the door. She peeped through the peephole and saw Prashant standing outside the door. Prashant was back home from Pune. She opened the door and let him in.

"Welcome dear," Pratima said while taking his bag from his hand. Prashant had gone to Pune to confirm Akash's admission for N.A.T.A. classes and hostel. The hostel and the classes were in the neighbourhood.

It was the first day of Akash's summer holidays and he was very much excited about it. Again he was in his plain formal clothes with flattened oily hair. As he reached down for breakfast, he saw Prashant and Pratima already at the table. Tejas was off to school as his ninth-standard exams were still on.

"When did you reach, papa?" Akash asked Prashant as he touched his feet for blessings.

"I reached today morning," Prashant said while Akash had his seat. "Now listen to me. You have to appear for N.A.T.A. before your admission to Architecture College. And for that, there is a coaching class called 'Mane's classes' in Pune. It is starting from the first of April. And opposite it, there is a Maratha Hostel where one of my friends' son – Amit is staying. I have done your admission at both places."

"But what is N.A.T.A.?" Akash asked.

"Its full form is – National Aptitude Test for Architecture. It's a kind of entrance exam. I will give you Amit's mobile number." Prashant said. "And this one is for you." Prashant removed a box from under the table. Akash saw that it was a mobile phone.

"Mobile phone!" Akash got excited. "Thank you, papa."

"Use it wisely," Prashant said. So, Akash had his breakfast and went out to show his new mobile phone to his friends.

"Hey guys, see what I have," Akash said while showing them his new phone.

"Even we have got new phones," Dhaval said and so, everyone showed their phones to each other. They even exchanged their contact numbers.

"By the way where are you all going to do your graduation?" Akash asked.

"Everyone is staying in over here, but I am going to Pune," Dhaval said.

"Oh! That's great. Even I am going to Pune on 29th March." Akash said.

"Why so early?" Ankita asked.

"I have to attain my entrance exams classes," Akash said.

"Nice. You guys will be having fun in Pune." Nitya said.

"Yeah, but I am not getting any chance to enjoy the holidays." Akash seemed disappointed.

"Even we are having classes over here. At least you will be there in a bigger city during your classes." Manish said.

"When are you coming to Pune?" Akash asked Dhaval.

"I will be reaching Pune in mid-June," Dhaval said. "In which area your hostel is?"

"I don't know," Akash said.

"And where are your classes?" Dhaval asked.

"I have no idea," Akash said.

"Then what do you know?" Dhaval asked. "You are not going to Pune for some vacation. Now try to keep more information about where you go."

Akash felt a bit awkward. But he thought for a while about Dhaval's words and realized that he was right. "Where are you going to stay?" He asked Dhaval.

"Papa has seen a hostel in Kothrud I guess," Dhaval said. Then they started playing their games. Akash happily spent his holidays with his friends. Then, the day arrived when he had to leave for Pune.

Pratima was helping him pack his luggage. She was upset and crying from within for getting separated from her son, but she did not want to show. Then, in the evening, Akash took Prashant's and Pratima's blessings before leaving. Pratima hugged and kissed him. "Take care and call us every day," Pratima said.

"Yes maa. Bye." Akash said. Then, he even hugged Tejas and left along with Prashant. Tejas had noticed unfallen tears in Pratima's eyes. But he couldn't say a word.

Then, on the next day, Akash and Prashant had reached Pune. They got down at the Shivaji Nagar bus stop and hired a rickshaw towards Akash's hostel.

"Take us to Tilak Road," Prashant said to the rickshaw driver. So, Akash learned that his classes and hostel were on Tilak Road. As they reached the hostel, they got down and saw the hostel's name written above the entrance gate – *Maratha Boys' Hostel.* Prashant paid the rickshaw driver and called Amit down.

"Good morning uncle." Amit wished Prashant happily as he reached down. He touched his feet and took his blessings.

"Good morning beta. How are you?" Prashant asked.

"I am fine," Amit said while picking up Prashant's luggage. But Prashant tried to stop him by saying, "Why are you taking the trouble?"

"It's all right uncle. Come inside." Amit said and took them up. Prashant went to the hostel's management's office to complete the formalities while Akash went along with Amit towards their room.

"This is our room," Amit said while taking Akash inside the room. Akash saw there were four beds in the room, each having a cupboard and a side table. Amit placed Akash's bag on one of the beds and said, "And this is your bed."

"Thank you bhaiya," Akash said. He saw that Amit was a charming and friendly boy. He was eight years older than him and was doing a job in a multinational company. Akash was very excited about big city life, but somewhere he was nervous about how he would manage without his parents.

"You get fresh. We will have breakfast on the ground floor and then I will show you your class." Amit said. Then, two boys entered the room. They were Sahil and Rishabh, their two roommates who were of the same age as Amit.

"So, the newcomer is here," Sahil said. "I am Sahil and this is Rishabh."

"Hello." Akash wished them.

"Your father is calling you down," Sahil said. So, Akash immediately went down. He saw his father waiting at the entrance lobby.

"Did you call me, papa?" Akash asked.

"All set?" Prashant asked.

"Yes, papa."

"Now I must leave, son," Prashant said with a heavy heart. He wanted to say – *I will miss you, son* to Akash. But that would discourage him. He just kissed his forehead and said, "Take care of yourself and be regular at your class. Don't forget to call your mother every day and keep you're A.T.M. card safe." Then, Akash took Prashant's blessings and said his farewell.

"Bye beta," Prashant said and started moving out while trying to hide his unfallen tears. Then, Akash went up and called Pratima to inform her that he had reached Pune and Prashant had left for Dhran by S.T. bus. Then, Akash got ready for the breakfast.

By the time Akash reached the dining hall on the ground floor, he saw that Amit, Sahil, and Rishabh were already there. Akash joined them. He saw that the dining hall was too huge. Then, their breakfast plate arrived which had mendu wadas with coconut chutney and sambar and a steel glass of tea. Akash's mouth got watery as he loved South Indian breakfast. He was going on ordering more menu wadas and coconut chutney while Amit, Rishabh, and Sahil just looked on. After their breakfast, he went to see his classes along with Amit.

Amit was a very jolly person who seemed very much excited about being with Akash. "It seems you liked the breakfast very much." He said to Akash while they were on their way towards his classes.

"Yes. It was really good." Akash said.

"You will like even the lunch and the dinner," Amit said. He showed him his classes which were exactly on the opposite side of the road. Then soon, they were back in their room. Sahil and Rishabh were ready to leave for their job. Even Amit got ready.

"Go and have a walk outside for today or else if you want, you can watch movies on my computer," Amit said to Akash and so, he spent his day that way. He even read the newspaper and saw the advertisement for the historic movie – *Jodha Akbar* he was excited about.

The next morning, the alarm rang. Akash woke up and dismissed the alarm at 6:30 AM. It was his first day at his class and as usual, he didn't want to be late. He furtively got ready, had his breakfast, and moved toward his class with just a notebook and a pen.

Akash had reached his classes fifteen minutes prior. He waited in the lobby. He was the first one to reach over there. His heart was pounding as if trying to break his ribs. He was getting nervous. He was flummoxed whether he was supposed to carry more books or not. Then, he saw a boy enter the lobby. He too was just carrying a book and a pen. He just gave a hint of a smile to Akash and sat next to him. "Hello." He said.

"Hi," Akash replied with a smile.

"From which college are you?" The boy asked in a friendly manner.

"Actually, I am not from Pune. I am from Dhran." Akash said.

"Okay." The boy said. "What's your name?"

"Akash Sharma," Akash replied. "And yours?"

"Shreyas Deshmukh." The boy said. Soon, all the students had arrived. The peon opened the classroom and so, the students moved inside and had their seats. Then immediately, Professor Ajit Mane arrived and the class began.

The day had passed. Amit had returned to the hostel in the evening along with Sahil and Rishabh. "How was your class?" He asked.

"It was good," Akash said. "Do you know any stationery shop nearby?"

"Tomorrow I am free. We will buy your stuff tomorrow." Amit said. "We three are planning to watch the *Jodha Akbar* movie tomorrow. You join us if you are free."

"Yeah, sure," Akash said as he was already excited for the historic movie. Then his phone rang. Akash saw that it was Prashant's call. He had a good talk with his both parents about his first day at the classes and the next day's movie plan. Prashant and Pratima both were happy to realize that their son was happy.

CHAPTER TWO

The next morning, Akash, Amit, Sahil, and Rishabh got ready. They had their breakfast and went to watch the movie in a multiplex. Akash was already excited about the movie, but he got more eager to see the multiplex for the first time. As they entered the screen room after buying their tickets, Akash gave an expression of 'WOW!' with wide-open eyes. He was startled to see such a huge room with countless seats and a huge screen. He had never seen such a huge theatre earlier.

"Did you like it?" Rishabh asked Akash while moving towards their seats.

"Yeah," Akash said. "Why don't we sit over here?" He added while pointing towards the empty seats near them from where they were passing.

"Dude, over here we have seat numbers. It's not like Dhran over here that you sit anywhere just below the fan." Amit said. Then they found their seats and sat over there. Akash was again amazed to have an experience of foldable cushion seats.

"This is still nothing. In the last row, there are recliners. It gets converted into a semi-bed so that we can lie on it and watch the movie." Amit said as he saw Akash's expression on his face.

"Wow!" Akash expressed.

"But we cannot afford it. It's charged two hundred and fifty rupees for one seat." Amit said.

"Two hundred and fifty rupees!" Akash was startled. "What is the cost of this seat on which we are sitting?"

"One hundred and twenty rupees," Amit said and so, Akash was again shocked. It was Amit who had bought the tickets for the four. Sahil and Rishabh had given him the amount. Now, Akash had to shell out rupees one hundred and twenty which seemed too much for him. He had seen theatres in Dhran having metal seats for not more than rupees fifty. Then, the lights went off and the national anthem started followed by the movie.

The movie ended after almost two and a half hours. Akash was very much satisfied after watching his most awaited movie. As they came out, Amit told Sahil and Rishabh, "You both carry on. I am taking Akash to A.B.C. to buy his stationery."

"Okay." Rishabh and took Sahil along.

"What does A.B.C. mean?" Akash asked with a baffled look.

"A.B.C. means Appa Balwant chowk." Amit said. Then he took out his bike and they started riding.

"Did you like the movie?" Amit asked.

"I was eagerly waiting for this movie since prior to my exams," Akash said. "Indian history is my favorite."

"Is it?" Amit asked.

"Yes." Akash said. He seemed to like his new life in a new city. Or maybe he was too fast to judge his new life. Then, they had reached Appa Balwant chowk which was a crowded area in the old city. Akash saw that the area was too congested with heavy traffic blowing continuous horn on road and pedestrian on the footpath. There was even some encroachment done by the *tapriwalas* on the footpath.

Then, after a prolong search, they found a parking space for their bike.

Akash saw that more than half of the shops on both the sides of the road were of stationery. They entered one of the shops which seemed luxurious. Akash was amazed to see such a posh stationery shop.

"This is Bharat traders. It is a stationery franchise. They have many outlets throughout Pune." Amit said. The shop was divided in various sections. Akash looked around and was shocked to see various types of paper sheets, cardboard sheets, various type of pens and pencils, colouring materials, registers, books, etc. "Over here, you will find everything you will require in your college. You just go to the required section, take your stuff to the counter and pay the bill." Amit added.

Akash had the list of what he had to buy for his classes. So, he bought everything, paid the bill and left the shop. He even gave the movie ticket amount to Amit.

Akash's days were well spent in the beginning. He would attend his classes in the morning and complete his assignments by afternoon. "What do you do in the evening?" Sahil asked during their dinner.

"Nothing." Akash said.

"What do you mean by 'nothing'?" Rishabh asked. "Go and roam in the city. You will get to know many new things. You have time right now, utilise it."

"You must be having friends at your classes, don't you?" Amit said. "Take them along." Akash got a bit confused. His only good friend was Shreyas, but he didn't know where he stayed and what he did in free time. It was only Amit, who would help him explore the city, but that too only during weekends.

Akash's entrance exam was declared. He immediately called his mother to give her the news. Pratima asked him about his preparation and so he assured her that he was well prepared for the test.

"Everytime you say that you are prepared, but your results are always opposite." Pratima taunted him. Prashant was hearing their conversation. "Pass the phone to me." He said to Pratima. Even Prashant had a talk with him and told him that he would book his bus tickets for the same day when his exam were over.

Akash was fully prepared for his exams. That early morning, Akash called Pratima and Prashant and took their blessings. Then after his breakfast, he straightaway went to his exam which ended after two hours. All the students were told to wait in the lobby as their exams sheets were being checked by the external examiner. Akash was getting nervous. "How was your exam?" He asked Shreyas.

"It was good. Let us see what the results are." Shreyas said. He too seemed a bit nervous. Then, after more than an hour, the students were called inside. Their results were ready. Akash's heartbeat was rising. He looked at Shreyas who just gave him a 'thumbs – up' sign. The students horded near the examiner's table and collected the results according to their names. Then, Akash got his result and he saw that he had passed. He took a sigh of relief. Everyone from his batch had passed. While on his way towards his hostel, he called his mother to herald her about his result.

"That's good. So, are you leaving tonight?" Pratima asked.

"Yes maa." Akash said. "See you tomorrow."

Akash had already packed his luggage. He was very much excited to go home. His bus would leave from Shivaji nagar at nine o'clock. While having dinner prior to leaving, many of his mates asked about where was he about to leave, as they saw him with his bag. He was answering everyone excitedly that he was going home.

Afterwards, Amit had dropped Akash at the bus stop at Shivaji nagar on his bike. People, who were travelling, had horded the area. Akash did not have to pay for the ticket as Prashant had already paid for it from Dhran. He had to wait for the bus as he had reached early. He was getting nervous as he was travelling alone for the first time. Then, the bus arrived.

"Okay bhaiya,see you soon." Akash said.

"Call me once you reach." Amit said.

"Sure." Akash said and started climbing up. But as he entered the bus, he realised that he did not know his berth number. The conductor was yet to come. He wanted to move out, but he was blocking other passengers' way, who were entering the bus after him.

"What's wrong with you?" The man standing behind him, asked in his heavy voice.

"Actually I want to ask my berth number to the conductor." Akash said hesitantly.

"First move on side and let us enter." The man said arrogantly. So, Akash kept his suitcase on the berth next to him and sat over there.

"Child, that's my berth." The man said again. This time he was controlling his anger.

"I am so sorry." Akash said nervously and moved to another berth. He saw that the people had started hording in the gangway, some searching their berths while some occupying theirs.

"Excuse me." A young lady said politely to Akash. "This is my berth."

"Oh! I am sorry." Akash said and moved towards the backside. He was getting more nervous. Then, as the gangway got cleared, he moved out and asked the conductor his berth number. The conductor asked his name, saw the passengers' list and confirmed his berth number. He even handed him the ticket and guided him towards his berth. After occupying his berth, he called his parents and told them that he had sat in the bus.

Next morning, Akash was about to reach Dhran. His nervousness was increasing. He stood up and moved towards the driver's cabin and asked about how much time was left to reach Dhran.

"We will take at least one hour to reach." The conductor said.

"I want to get down at Sardar Patel Chowk." Akash said.

"Okay." The conductor said and so, Akash went back to his berth. After sometime, Akash again went to the conductor and said, "Don't forget to stop at Sardar Patel Chowk in Dhran."

"Yes, I know." The conductor said. Again Akash went to his place. He was continuously looking out of the windshield to get a hint of reaching Dhran. But there seemed no sign. Then, his phone rang. He saw that it was Pratima's call. She was asking him about his location, but he didn't have any idea.

Akash again waited for sometime. But then, he couldn't resist. He again stood up and went to the driver's cabin. "Bhaiya,please do stop at Sardar Patel Chowk."

"Dude I know where you want to get down." The conductor got frustrated. "Now you go and sit at your place." So, Akash went back to his place out of chagrin. Then, after sometime, Akash saw the huge entrance gate of Dhran. He immediately called Prashant and told him to reach at Sardar Patel Chowk.

Akash was seeing his home-town after almost two months. He was getting more exited. He eagerly took his suitcase and got up to move towards the driver's cabin. But he saw the conductor entering and announcing, "Sardar Patel Chowk. Sardar Patel Chowk." He came to Akash and said, "Your destination has arrived."

The bus halted at Sardar Patel chowk and so, Akash excitedly climbed down. The bus went away and Akash saw Prashant riding his scooter towards him.

"Good morning, son." Prashant said with a big smile. He seemed very happy for his son's return.

"Good morning, papa." Akash said while taking his blessings. Then, they both moved towards their home.

While on their way, Akash was happily seeing the surrounding locality, filling him with nostalgia. He was out of the town for almost just two months, but it felt like ages. He was familiar with the area since his childhood, but still it felt new to him. Then, they entered the lane where their house was. At far end Akash saw his house. He was filed with joy. He had finally reached his home – sweet home.

"Ting-tong." The doorbell rang. Pratima furtively scooted in excitement towards the door to open it as she knew her son had returned. She saw Akash and Prashant standing outside.

"Welcome, my boy." Pratima said while hugging Akash for a while. Then, Akash touched her feet for blessings. "How are you maa?" He asked.

"I am fine. How is my son?" Pratima asked.

"I am fine too." Akash replied happily.

"Now let us enter and then have your talks." Prashant said while towing Akash's suitcase inside.

"Go and get fresh. I will get your breakfast ready." Pratima said. So, Akash immediately went up to his bedroom and met Tejas over there.

"Hey, how are you?" Akash asked Tejas while hugging him.

"I am good bhaiya. What about you?" Tejas asked.

"I am good too." Akash said. Soon, he got ready and went down to have his breakfast. As soon as Akash reached the dining hall, he was surprised to see two sugar parathas basted with sugar syrup and a bowl of fresh cream in his plate. "Wow!" He exclaimed.

"Just look at how much she is happy on seeing his son come back." Prashant taunted.

"I knew you would say this line." Pratima said while bringing the frying pan on the dining table. "So, this is for you." She said while flipping the paratha from the pan to his plate.

After the breakfast, Akash went out to join his colony friends. Akash was too excited to meet his friends. Everyone was amazed to see him. They all had a good talk together. They even asked him about his exams.

"Don't ask that. I have passed, that's it." Akash said. Everyone understood what he meant and so, they all had a guffaw.

"How were your days in Pune?" Minakshi asked.

"All of my days got spend behind my classes and studies." Akash said.

"Yeah but still you must have enjoyed something, haven't you?" Nitya asked.

"I would not get time for that." Akash said dumbly.

"You were there in Pune for more than two months and you are saying that you didn't explore the city!" Dhaval said as he was shocked. Akash just gave him a blank look. "Man, you really need to organise your time-table. You really don't know what you have missed."

The days went on. Then, Akash's twelfth standard board exams' results were declared. "There is good news. Akash has scored sixty one percent in his exams." Prashant announced happily as he had check the result online.

"Is it?" Pratima asked as she got excited. Even Akash and Tejas had got happy on hearing the result.

"I will go and collect the result from the college." Akash said. So, he got ready and immediately went to his college along with his friends. While on their way, they had a good discussion about their results.

As Akash and his friends reached their college, they saw all the students hoarding in the ground. They even saw his ex-classmates over there and shared some happy words with them. Then, the principal arrived.

"Good morning everyone." The principal announced. "Today, your results are out. By this time, I hope you all have decided your career. Some will be doctors, some will be engineers, some will be doing business, etc." The students were not at all interested in listening to the principal. But they did not have any choice.

"Why is there any need for him to give such a boring lecture?" Manish nudged Akash and asked in a low voice.

"Everyone has already seen their results online. He should have just distributed the hard copies and end it." Akash replied in the same way.

"Some of you have scored very well. I pray that you continue to score well and achieve your goals in future. But there are many of you who need to struggle a lot. Now, your class teacher will hand over your results to you." The principal added. So, everyone moved towards their respective classes.

The class teacher distributed the results. Akash and his friends had collected their results. Some were in Science stream along with him while some were in Commerce. They saw their results and started moving towards their homes.

As Akash reached his home, Pratima saw his result and said, "Your father has said that you need to go to Pune tonight. You should fill your admission forms as soon as possible."

"Okay." Akash replied.

"Do you know any college for architecture?" Pratima asked.

"No." Akash said randomly.

"As expected." Pratima said in distress. "What were you doing for two months over there?"

"I had classes to attain." Akash said.

"Yeah, but still you should have found out some colleges. Your father has told Amit to accompany you tomorrow." Pratima said. Then Akash went to his bedroom to get his luggage ready.

In the evening, Akash got ready to leave for Pune. He touched Pratima's feet and said good bye to her and Tejas and left along with Prashant towards the bus stop.

Next morning, as Akash reached Pune, he got down at Shivaji Nagar bus stop. Amit had come to receive him. Firstly, he congratulated him for his result and then, they moved. "I have shortlisted some architecture colleges for you. First we will get fresh at our hostel, have our breakfast and then visit the colleges." Amit said.

"But bhaiya, you will get disturbed, won't you?" Akash said.

"Don't worry, I have taken leave for today." Amit said. Soon, they had reached their hostel. Akash met Sahil and

Rishabh in their room. Soon, he and Amit got ready, had their breakfast and went to the colleges.

"First, we will go to Shivneri College as it seems good one." Amit said.

"Where is it?" Akash asked.

"It's far away, on the outskirts of Pune on S. G. Road." Amit said and started riding the bike. Akash was enjoying the long ride. They were passing through the areas which were new to him. The malls, shopping complexes and residential societies amazed him a lot. Then, after a long time, they had finally reached Shivneri College. They had to park the bike in the visitors parking area just outside the campus. Then, as they entered the campus, Akash was startled, "Wow, such a huge campus!"

"Amazing, isn't it?" Amit said. Akash saw that the campus was immense and full of students, out of which some were applying for admission while some were already staying over there in the hostel and attending their college. He even saw that the campus had various buildings of different colleges like business management, medical, dental, law, engineering, hotel management, fashion designing, etc. After crossing half a kilometer, they had finally reached the architecture college. It was quite huge building.

As they entered the college building, they straight away went to the office and asked the admission process on the counter. The staff handed them the form and told them to attach all the required documents with it. He even guided them towards the head of the department's cabin. As they entered the cabin, they were shocked to see its huge and luxurious interior. They saw the H.O.D. on his table at far end. He was viewing some documents.

"May we come in, sir?" Amit asked. The H.O.D. raised his head and saw both of them at the entrance.

"Yes." He said arrogantly. So, they both walked towards the table and had their seats. The H.O.D. seemed snobbish by the way he looked at them.

"Sir, actually we wanted to ask about the procedure for admission in architecture." Amit said.

"Just fill the form and wait for our call. If you are selected, then pay the fees. That's it." The H.O.D. snapped bluntly while continuing his work.

"Sir, what will be the fees?" Amit asked.

"Rupees one lakh for one year, neither less nor more." The H.O.D. said.

"Okay, thank you." Amit said and started walking out with Akash. "The H.O.D. is too arrogant and doesn't seem to be interested." He said to Akash.

"So, should we try for this college or not?" Akash asked.

"The fee is too high. Let me talk to your father, and then we will decide." Amit said.

Amit and Akash had visited all the colleges throughout the day. All the colleges had almost the same fee structure. But still, they had filled the forms over there. Then, at the end, they had reached K.B.H. College of architecture. It also had a huge campus having various colleges in it. As usual, they collected the admission form and met the H.O.D. Over there, they came to know that the admission list would be closing at sixty percent and the fee was Rupees thirty five thousand for first year.

Amit and Akash had realised that the K.B.H. College was much preferable in terms of fees and closing admission list. Even it was just a kilometer away from their hostel. Amit even had a talk with Prashant and assured him that it was a reputed college.

"Okay, then go for it." Prashant said. So, they filled the admission form over there.

Next day, Akash had reached Dhran. As earlier, Prashant had reached at Sardar Patel chowk to receive him. He asked Akash about his admission process and so, he told him that he was sure about K.B.H. Then, they had reached home. Over there, Akash had same talks with Pratima.

Akash was staying at his home since days, enjoying his holidays with his friends while waiting from the calls from the colleges. Tejas' tenth standard classes had already started.

It was in the beginning of July 2008. It was a fine morning. As usual, Akash got ready and reached down for breakfast when his mobile phone rang. He saw that it was an unknown number. But still he received it. "Hello." He said and paused for a while, while listening to the other person. "Okay, thank you." He added and cut the call.

"Who was it?" Pratima asked.

"The call was from K.B.H. College. They are saying that I am eligible for the admission and we are supposed to pay the fees by this week." Akash said.

"That's a good news." Pratima said anxiously.

"Let me talk to Amit." Prashant said and called Amit.

"Good morning uncle." Amit said as he received the call.

"Good morning beta." Prashant said. "Can you please do me a favour? Akash needs to pay his college fees at K.B.H. College. Just now he had a call from the college. So, will you be able to go and pay it? I will transfer the money in your account." Prashant said.

"Okay uncle, no problem. I will do it." Amit said and cut the call.

Next morning, when Prashant was about to leave for his shop, he got a call from Amit stating that he had paid the fees and the college was about to start from 28th of July.

"Okay beta. Thank you very much." Prashant said.

"It's my pleasure, uncle." Amit said and cut the call. Then, Prashant called Pratima and Akash and gave the good news. On hearing this, Pratima got excited and kissed Akash's forehead. But Akash had mixed feelings. He was excited as well as nervous. He was doubtful whether he would be able to do architecture or not.

CHAPTER THREE

On 28th of July 2008, Akash had got ready for his college and had reached the bus stop. He had reached Pune a day earlier. Amit had guided him about the buses, but still he was a bit bemused as he was travelling in the city bus for the first time. Even after entering the bus, he just stood near the exit.

"Move inside, boy. You are blocking the way." The conductor bid. So he moved inside just a couple of feet as he was about to reach his destination.

"I want to get down at K.B.H. College. Please let me know when my stop will arrive." Akash said.

"Your stop is about to come." The conductor said. Then, the bus halted and Akash got down. He had reached K.B.H. College. He looked up at campus entrance gate which had the campus name – K.B.H. Campus written above it. He entered the campus and walked towards the college. As he reached the college building, he saw the students hoarding outside it. The gate was still closed. He too waited over there.

"Akash." He heard someone calling him from behind. He turned around and to his surprise, he saw Shreyas over there.

"Hey, how are you?" Akash asked.

"I am fine. I can't believe you are here." Shreyas said. "When is the gate going to open?"

"I don't know. I too reached just now." Akash said. They waited for a while over there, swapping their stories of their summer vacation. Then, they saw a peon coming to the gate and unlocking it. As the gate got opened, all the students started entering the building. Akash and Shreyas followed them. Akash was amazed to see the building. It had a huge central courtyard with a stage on one side. The classes were on its either sides. The students were moving towards the first floor. As they reached their class, Akash saw the board on the entrance with F.Y.B. Arch. written on it. But as soon as he entered it, he was astonished to see its huge size. He had not seen such a huge class like that earlier. He entered the class and had his seat just in front of Shreyas.

Akash seemed excited as a new chapter in his life was getting started. But in no time, the principal – Professor Abhishek Dhakad arrived along with the class teacher – Professor Aishwarya Deshmukh. Everyone stood up to greet them. "Sit down." Professor Dhakad said while having his seat. Professor Deshmukh stood beside him. Professor Dhakad seemed to be in his fifty's. Firstly, he introduced himself and Professor Deshmukh to the class and gave all the important information regarding the college and the campus to the students. Then he gave a lecture, introducing architecture to everyone.

Professor Dhakad continued his lecture for around an hour. Everyone in the class was getting bored. Akash looked around and saw that everyone just seemed pretending to be attentive. Then, the principal ended his lecture and handed over the class to professor Deshmukh.

Professor Deshmukh was a young lady who was supposed to teach them Architectural Design. But as it was the first day, she could just introduce the subject.

The first day went quite well with no assignments at all. Only introduction of the subjects were given out of which, some of them were not understood by Akash.

By noon, as Akash reached his hostel, he had his lunch and went to his room. Then he called his mother to talk to her about his fine day at the college.

After the call, he took Amit's laptop computer and started watching the historic movie of Akbar and Jodha. Amit had bought the movie's C.D. a few days back.

In the evening, Amit, Sahil and Rishabh had returned from their offices. "So how was your day?" Amit asked Akash.

"It was good." Akash said. "Bhaiya, can you please come with me to the stationery shop? I want to buy things from there."

"For this, you waited for me since afternoon!" Amit said as he was shocked.

"Yes." Akash replied impulsively.

"You should have hired a bus or an auto-rickshaw. You know the place." Amit said. Akash was at loss of words out of chagrin. It was such a small thing to buy the stationery which he couldn't do alone.

"You can do one thing. Ask your father to buy a bike for you. You will be over here for five years. You will need it very often." Sahil said. But Akash couldn't reply him.

"Okay, let's go." Amit said and moved out. Akash followed him. He had the list of sheets, tracing papers, different types of pencils and pens, T – square, set square, sheet containers, and much more. Then, they had reached Bharat traders' shop.

As earlier, Akash was amazed to see the posh interior of the shop. They didn't want to waste time as they were getting late for dinner. While collecting the things from the shop, Amit saw that it seemed too costly. "Is it necessary to buy such costly things?" He asked Akash.

"Actually we are told to buy all this stuff." Akash said. They furtively collected everything on the checklist and moved towards the billing counter. But, as the man on the counter handed them the bill, Akash was startled to see the final amount. It was rupees two thousand one hundred and fifty three. Akash had never bought stationery costing so much. He just had fifteen hundred rupees in his wallet.

"See, I told you." Amit said. "I will pay it today. You can return me tomorrow, but next time be careful." He added while paying the amount. Then they left the shop.

"Shall I talk to papa for a scooter?" Akash asked.

"Give it a try." Amit said. Then, they moved towards their hostel. After the dinner, as Akash reached his room, he called Prashant to talk about the scooter.

"I was thinking so." Prashant said. He paused for a second and added. "I will buy you a scooter."

"Thank you papa." Akash said happily.

The conversation was heard by Pratima. "Prashant, first let him settle over there. Let him learn how to travel and adjust in the crowed city buses."

"Pratima, he has to carry his sheets and card-board models to college. How will he be able to carry it in crowded buses?" Prashant said. But Pratima couldn't answer.

Next day, Akash had got ready to leave for his college. But, on seeing him carrying everything what they had bought the day earlier, Amit said, "Why are you carrying everything?"

"We are told to bring all this to the college." Akash said while wearing his shoes.

"Are you sure? Because how will you carry this huge container in the bus?" Amit asked.

"I don't know. Let's see." Akash said and left. He had reached the bus stop. But as the bus arrived, he saw that the bus was heavily crowded. He got tensed, but he lacked time. So, somehow he managed to climb the bus. There was no space in the bus to stand properly. It was very difficult for him to carry his luggage.

"You should have hired an auto-rickshaw if you had this much stuff to carry." The conductor taunted him. But he could just collect the ticket without uttering a word. He wondered whether everyday he had to face all this or not. He wished if his father would send him his new scooter at the earliest. His stop was nearing. So, he had to shove everyone on his way towards the exit. Some of the passengers were yelling at him, but he turned a deaf-ear to them. He somehow got down from the bus and managed to reach his college. His shoulders had started aching because of his boulder-like-bag. But, as he enter the class, he was shocked to see everyone with materials less than half of what he had.

"Why have you brought all this stuff?" Shreyas asked.

"We were told to bring all this, weren't we?" Akash said. Everyone was goggling at him and murmuring about him after seeing him with the huge rectangular sheet container and a heavy bag.

"We were given everyday schedule yesterday. Anyways, let it be." Shreyas said. Akash had his seat while in chagrin for his absentmindedness. He was afraid that his behavior would create his negative image in front of everyone over here, just like in Dhran. Then, professor Deshmukh arrived and the class began.

The college was over by afternoon. After reaching hostel, he had his lunch and then, went to his room and called his mother to inform her about the day. Pratima was pleased to know that he was happy in his new college.

In the evening, as Amit returned back along with Sahil and Rishabh, he said to Akash, "Your father had called me. He has bought a scooter for you. Tomorrow morning, it will reach Pune."

"Oh really!" Akash said excitedly. He immediately called Prashant and thanked him for the vehicle. Prashant gave him the transporter's address and bid him to collect the vehicle the next day. He even told him to take care of the vehicle's documents which were in the trunk.

"Okay papa, it will be done. Thank you very much." Akash said with his happiness knowing no boundaries.

Next day, after returning from the college, Akash straight away went to the address of the transporter to collect his new scooter. It was in Shivaji Nagar. Amit had explained him the address and had guided him how he would reach. But still he had to ask the location to a lot of people over there. He had even called the transporter to guide him but he couldn't understand it properly. Then somehow, after sometime he managed to reach the destination. Over there, he confirmed his name and all the required details on the counter. Then, two men brought his scooter from inside, completely wrapped in plastic. Akash got filled with joy. He finally had a new scooter. The men got the scooter on the road, unwrapped it and handed the keys to him. He opened the trunk and saw the insurance certificate, the registration certificate, and the road tax receipt kept in a plastic bag in it. Then he called his father and heralded him that he had received the scooter. Then he excitedly rode off to his hostel.

The next day was Akash's first day at college on his new scooter. He had expected everyone to congratulate him for his new ride. But as usual, none responded. Even Shreyas had turned a blind-eye to him and he was used to it. He wished for a chance to meet his childhood friends and show them his new scooter. At least they would have been happy for him. He wished he could rewind his time so that he would be along with his childhood friends.

The days went on. Akash used to go to college on his new scooter and tried his level best to cope with the assignments. But, the more he tried, the more it was getting difficult for him. All his classmates were able to pick up the pace while he always ended up being a dawdler. By this, no one wanted to befriend him. Even he tried to join Shreyas' friends group. But no one responded him.

For assignment's submission, everyone in the class would help each other but Akash just had himself with him. When everyone used to have five-to-six sheets for class presentation, he would just have two-to-three sheets that too sometimes without its borders masked with tape. When everyone would have proper models for their designs, he would have one without finishing touch.

"Everyday, you are just with your stuff. Why don't you take out some time and go out with your friends?" Amit used to ask this very often on seeing him struggle with his assignments. But he had no words to share as he had no friends to be with. The only good friends he had in Pune was Dhaval. He was doing well in his life. But he stayed so far, it wasn't possible for Akash to meet him more than once every three months.

Then, Akash's first semester exams were nearing. Before that, their internal submissions were declared. Everyone had to make portfolios of the drawing sheets they had made of all the subjects throughout the semester.

On the first day, Akash readied his first portfolio and the models and took it to his college. That day, they had to show Architectural Drawing's portfolio. He was quite confident about his portfolio. But as he reached his classroom, he was left startled. Everyone had a portfolio and models made much better then him.

"Why couldn't you complete your models?" A girl asked him.

"I thought this would be enough." Akash said nervously.

"But we are having marks for this." The girl said. But he couldn't answer her. Out of chagrin, he walked towards his desk and kept his portfolio and models on it. The on-lookers stared at him and muttered about his presentation, but he tried to avoid it. Then Professor Deshmukh arrived and started inspecting the presentations.

By afternoon, Akash had reached his hostel. Professor Deshmukh had defamed him in front of the whole class because of his incomplete work, which left him completely perturbed. He didn't know why that was happening to him. He couldn't even consume his food that day. Just by killing his unfallen tears in his eyes, he tried to work on his next day's portfolio.

The internal submissions had ended. All the portfolios of Akash were the same, incomplete and untidy. Because of that, he had scored not much in his internal marking. Now, his only hope was his first semester exams which were to happen within few days.

While most of the students in his class were completely prepared for the exams, Akash was trying to complete all his remaining work regarding his portfolio and models. But, still he was not feeling confident. Then, his phone rang. He saw that it was Pratima's call. "Hello maa." He said.

"How is my son doing?" Pratima asked.

"Everything is good." Akash quavered.

"But it doesn't seem so." Pratima said. "What are you trying to hide?"

"It's nothing. Just the exam's pressure." Akash explained.

"Everything is going to be fine. Just give your best." Pratima said.

"Thank you maa, bye."

After somedays, Akash's first semester exams had occurred. As he reached his college, he saw that everyone was confidently discussing about their drawing with each other. But none was interested in his drawing. Even Shreyas had started avoiding him.

The students were waiting in the corridor outside the classroom. Then, everyone saw a lady arriving and entering the class along with Professor Deshmukh. She seemed to be the external examiner. Then, the students were called inside according to their roll number. The first student went inside the class with his portfolio and models. A total silence spread throughout the corridor. The next students seemed eager to know what was going inside the class. Even Akash's heartbeat was increasing. He didn't know how he would face the examiner. Then, almost after half an hour, the first student came out of the class. But, before even he would take his breadth, everyone gathered around him to know what he was asked. But Akash didn't join them.

The students entered and exited the exam hall according to their roll numbers. Everyone took around twenty-to-thirty minutes for their oral exam. Soon, Akash was the next one to enter the exam hall. He tried to hide his fear, but his efforts were in vein. Then, his name was called and he entered the hall.

Akash, after entering the exam hall, nervously placed his portfolio on the examiner's table. The examiner stared at his work with astonishment. "Is this all what you have?" She asked. She seemed a bit snobbish to him.

"Yes ma'am." He said edgily.

"Okay, explain all this to me." The examiner said and so, Akash opened his portfolio and started showing his drawings to her. Akash went on talking about his drawing and turning the sheets. He even showed her his models of the drawings. But she seemed to be not liking it. And within ten minutes, Akash had finished because of his incomplete work.

"Is it over?" The examiner asked.

"Yes ma'am." Akash said nervously. So, the examiner marked his work and let him go. As he was leaving the exam hall, he was expecting everyone to surround him and ask everything regarding the exam. But, it did not happen. Rather, one of them asked, "How come you finished so early?" But he could not answer him out of annoyance. Everyone was shocked to see him exit the exam hall so early. Seeing no one reacting to him, he placed his portfolio in the container and left for his hostel. He was deeply hurt from within but he suppressed his feeling, making his heart heavy.

After reaching his hostel, Akash wiped the unfallen tears out of his eyes and pretended to be normal. He tried his level best to prepare for his next exam. But there were some subjects like History of architecture and Theory of structures in which he didn't know what was he lacking. Even asking any help from his classmates was a futile notion. So, throughout the exams, he would just go to the exam hall with his incomplete stuff and finish it within ten minutes.

The first semester had ended. Akash had reached Dhran to spend his fifteen days' vacation. On the first day, when his parents had asked him about his exams, he had pretended that his exams were good. Then, he went out to meet his friends. Even Dhaval had come to Dhran.

Everyone was happy meeting each other after a long time. The first thing they chatted about was their exams. But Akash was least interested in the talks. "Why are we discussing about exams and marks? The exams are over." He said. Then, they started playing indoor games.

Soon, Akash's holidays were over. He had reached Pune on the first day of the second semester. He was worried about his result but still had made up his mind to apply full efforts for his next exams. He had reached his college before time as usual. His class mated were chattering about how they spend their holidays. But, he straight away went to his desk without a word with anyone. Even Shreyas was busy with his friends.

"Good morning everyone." Professor Aishwarya Deshmukh announced as she entered the class. Everyone stood alert and responded, "Good morning ma'am."

"Your results are out and you will be getting it today." Professor Deshmukh said while placing the results' bunch on the table. Akash got scared hearing that. He knew he wouldn't be getting good marks. He scanned the class and saw that everyone was a bit nervous, but not till the extent like him. Then the professor started distributing the results.

The students collected their results according to their roll numbers. Akash's heartbeat was increasing as his number was nearing. Then, Professor Deshmukh announced, "Akash Sharma." Akash bit his lips as he heard his name. He nervously stood up and walked towards Professor Deshmukh.

"What is wrong with you, Akash?" Professor Deshmukh asked. "Out of all seven subjects, you are failing in five." Akash got completely shaken from within after hearing that. Even everyone in his class was shocked. "I am calling you parents this Saturday." She added while handing the result to him.

After the college, when Akash had reached his hostel, he got a call from Pratima stating that she had a call from Professor Deshmukh regarding his result. Her temper was out of control.

"We were asking you about your preparations everyday, weren't we?" Pratima gave a pause and continued, "I am coming to Pune this Saturday. Your ma'am has called me." She ended the call after that.

Akash's confidence was completely broken. Then, Saturday had arrived. As usual, Akash had reached his college before time. He wanted to wait for his mother, but he didn't know when she would arrive. So, he straight away went to his class. While his History of Architecture's class was going on, a senior girl came to his class and told Professor Veena Chatterjee that Professor Aishwarya Deshmukh had called Akash in the staff room. Akash fell numb after hearing his name. He knew for what he was called. Professor Chatterjee granted him the permission and so, Akash went to the staff room. Over there, he saw his mother talking to Professor Deshmukh.

"May I come in ma'am?" Akash asked Professor Deshmukh. Pratima heard his voice and turned toward him as he was standing at the door.

"Yes, come in." Professor Deshmukh said. So, Akash walked inside and stood beside Pratima.

"Ma'am, as you know Akash is failing is five subjects and that is really a serious matter. The problem is, he is not at all attentive in the class. Neither he makes friends nor does he talk to anyone. He just sits aloof, completely lost in his own world." Professor Deshmukh said.

"Is it true, Akash?" Pratima asked while glowering at Akash. But Akash couldn't answer her.

"I have tried helping him out personally, but there are no efforts seen from his side." Professor Deshmukh said.

"What is all this Akash? Are you interested in architecture or not?" Pratima asked angrily. "Ask your classmates and your teachers if you don't understand anything."

"One semester is gone. But still, he has second semester to improve." Professor Deshmukh said.

"Ma'am, is his attendance perfect?" Pratima asked.

"Yes, it's above ninety percent. But what is the use of it when he is not mentally present?" Professor Deshmukh asked.

"Ma'am, pardon him this time. I will take care of him henceforth." Pratima said.

"Don't worry ma'am, I am always there to help him. But he has to make efforts. That's all." Professor Deshmukh said.

"Thank you ma'am." Pratima said and left the staff room, followed by Akash.

"Akash, are you serious or not regarding your career? Why do you stay aloof and don't make friends?" Pratima asked. "This is the last time I am tolerating this, I am warning you. Next time don't expect me to hear this complain, is that clear?"

"Yes maa." Akash said in a low voice. Then, Pratima left. She was staying at her friend – Janhvi's place in Pune.

Next morning, Pratima had reached Dhran. While having breakfast, Pratima was silent with a heavy heart.

Seeing her upset, Prashant asked, "What happened? What did Akash's professor said?"

Pratima took a deep breath and said, "Prashant, I think we have done a huge mistake regarding Akash's career."

• 35 •

CHAPTER FOUR

"Mistake in what sense?" Prashant asked curiously.

"I think Akash wasn't ready for Architecture." Pratima said in dismay.

"I had warned you earlier." Prashant said. "And nothing is easier, sweetheart. He has to learn to face difficulties. Now don't worry, everything is going to be fine." Prashant said and left for his shop.

Akash's second semester seemed to be the same as that of his first one. He would miss all the deadlines as usual in spite of spending his whole time on his work. He would go to college with his incomplete work while his classmates would submit better work than him. His teachers tried their level best to guide him, but their efforts were in vain.

Even at the end of the semester when his second-term exams had happened, he was prepared the same way as his first-term exam. And not to forget his one-and-a-half-month summer holidays in which he was supposed to learn new things and enjoy them to the fullest, he just spend them passing his time with his friends.

Then, Akash's result was declared in the last week of May. Like always, he had reached his college before time. He had to wait outside the main entrance as the main entrance was not yet opened.

"Akash." Akash heard Shreyas calling him. He was surprised. "How are you?" Shreyas added.

"I am fine. What about you?" Akash asked.

"I am good." Shreyas replied.

"How were your holidays?" Akash asked but suddenly, one of Shreyas' friends reached him.

"Hey, how are you?" Shreyas asked his friend and they started chatting. Akash felt offended as Shreyas again avoided him. He knew he would be forlorn forever. He just sat on the side bench and saw the students coming and hoarding near the entrance. Then, the entrance was opened and the students were called inside.

Everyone in the class was discussing their holidays with each other. But Akash just sat on his bench and avoided everyone. "Good morning everyone." Professor Deshmukh said as she entered the class. Everyone fell silent. Even Akash got tensed as he saw the bundle of results with her. He knew his exams were not good and he wasn't confident about passing.

Professor Deshmukh started calling everyone according to their roll number. And soon, Akash's name was called. Akash nervously stood up and started walking towards the professor. But as he received his result, he couldn't believe his eyes. He had passed in all of his subjects. He had just scored forty five percent, but he had cleared all of his subjects.

Next day, Akash had reached Dhran. His parents were very happy to learn that he had passed in all of his subjects.

In the next June, Akash's college had begun. He was promoted to second year. Again he tried to cope up with his assignments, but would fail to produce his work on time. Just like his previous year, his parents would receive complaints from his class teacher – Professor Vaishnavi Iyer. Day-by-day, his parents were getting perturbed for him.

His first semester exams had happened in which he had failed in a couple of subjects. But his second semester was much worst. He was failing four subjects. Akash's parents were too upset on seeing his performance. If he would have failed in one more subject, then he would have to repeat the whole year.

Somehow, Akash had managed to reach till his third year. But the situation for him was getting from bad to worst. The course of architecture was getting much tough for him and so, he was losing interest in it. After his first semester exams of third year, he had to appear to clear his subjects of second year in which he had failed.

After his exams, Akash had a half months' vacation. When he was in Dhran, he had come to know about two historic television shows. One was based on the life of the queen of Jhansi *Rani Laxmibai* and the other was based on the life of the first Maurya emperor *Chandragupt Maurya*. As Akash was in love with history, he would watch the shows everyday without fail.

Akash's second semester had begun. Even his first semester result was out. He had cleared all his subjects of second year but was failing in couple of subjects of his third year. This time, it was Professor Jinisha Agrawal who had called Pratima to college.

"Akash, this is getting on my nerves. I am asking you last time, are you interested in your course or not?" Pratima asked Akash after meeting Professor Agrawal. But Akash could not reply.

Akash was very much disappointed. He had become a joke in his class. He had started hating himself. He couldn't visualize anything regarding his future. He wished he could rewind his time since his S.S.C. days so that he could take admission along with his childhood friends and enjoy the moment.

Then, his second semester exams had happened which was tough as earlier exams. But Akash had got used to it. He was mentally prepared for failing in around three subjects as earlier. But as he received his result after a month of his exams, he was completely startled. He could not believe his eyes. He had failed in six subjects. He had lost his year.

"This was expected." Prashant said on seeing his result when Akash reached Dhran the next day. "Now what are you supposed to do?"

"I will have to appear for the exams in October." Akash said nervously with his head down.

"Akash, you have lost one whole year. Do you really realise what it is to lose a year?" Prashant threw the result card on the sofa angrily while Pratima looked at them from the corner. "For God's sake, now please try to be serious." Prashant warned Akash. Akash then looked at Pratima who was glaring at him in anger without any word.

Akash had brought all of his stuff to Dhran and cancelled his registration from his hostel. Prashant had told him to study from home for his October exams.

Then, Akash's October exams had arrived. During his exams, he was staying at Janhvi's place. As usual, he would reach his college before time. On the first day, he saw that there were very few of his classmates who were appearing for the exams along with him. Then, he saw Shreyas and all this other classmates who were one year ahead of him now. They had come for their first semester exam of their fourth year.

Akash felt bad for himself after seeing his old classmates ahead of him. He wanted to cry but he had to kill his feelings inside him. He always used to ask himself that why all that was happening to him.

Akash's October exams had ended and his results were out. Out of six subjects, he was still failing in four. He could take admission in fourth year in next June, but had to clear his remaining subjects in April exams. His parents were worried about him and so was he.

But the best part of his college life was yet to come. It was December 2011. All of his childhood friends had decided to have a grand get-together on the New Year's Eve. So, Akash got very much excited as they would be together after a long time.

It was 20th December. When Akash woke up in the morning, he took his phone to read the whatsapp chats. He saw Dhruv's message in his friends' group stating that he had reached Dhran. Akash got excited. He furtively got ready, had his breakfast and straight away went to Dhruv's place. Over there, they had a good chat. Then Dhruv asked him about his exams to which, he replied, "Don't ask me that." Akash said and so, they both had a guffaw. Then, they went out to call Minakshi and Nitya.

Akash, Nitya, Dhruv, and Minakshi had a good talk. Minakshi even japed that she always met Nitya but Akash didn't have time to meet. While playing her chance in ludo, she even asked Dhruv for how many days he was there. To that, Dhruv replied that he would be going back after the new-year party.

"I rarely go to college. So, they are used to my absentees." Dhruv said and so, everyone had a good laugh.

Akash and his friends continued playing for a long time. Then it was afternoon. "Now let us have our lunch. We shall meet in the evening." Akash said.

"First, let's take a selfie. We are meeting after a long time." Dhruv said while taking out his phone. Then, everyone gave a pose and he took the photo. Then, everyone winded the game and started moving toward their home. Akash had reached his home and immediately had his lunch. Then, he went to his bedroom for his studies. Then, in the evening, Dhruv called him and asked, "Shall we go to the khau-galli?"

"Yes, of course." Akash said. He immediately got ready and went downstairs. While he was moving out, Pratima asked him about his studies. So, he assured her that he would cover-up.

"Come back soon." Pratima said strictly. So, Akash went to join his friends.

Then, as soon as they reached the khau-galli, they were amazed to see it. It was newly constructed on the banks of river Phajran. It was having a wide road and a huge platform with seating arrangements facing the river.

"What shall we have?" Dhruv asked.

"Let us have soya bean chilli at stall number thirteen." Nitya said. "The Chinese dishes are good over there."

"Have you been over here?" Akash asked in amasement.

"Yeah."

"So, let us move to stall number thirteen." Minakshi said. So, they went there and took a table for four. Over there, they ordered a plate of soya bean chilli and paneer chilli.

"It's a really beautiful place." Dhruv said. "When did this started?"

"Around fifteen days back." Akash replied.

"By the way, when are others going to come?" Minakshi asked.

"After two days, Ankita and Rohan are coming. Dhaval is coming two days prior to the New Year's Eve. I don't know about Sejal and Manish." Dhruv said.

"We will visit here again with these guys." Minakshi said.

"Actually we are having a long list of places." Akash said.

"When is Tejas coming?" Nitya asked Akash.

"Within two-to-three days." Akash said. Then, the waiter brought the plates having soya bean chilli and paneer chilli. Akash's mouth was watering on seeing those dishes. But as he was about to grab his bite, Nitya interjected, "Wait. Let us take pictures first." So, they took pictures with their mobile camera and then started eating.

"This is awesome." Akash said after having some bites.

"The crowd you are seeing right now is nothing as compared to weekends. Today is Wednesday. That's why the crowd is less." Nitya said. Then, soon they had finished.

"There is a pedestrian bridge around half a kilometer away from here. It's from this bank of the river to the opposite bank." Nitya said.

"Pedestrian bridge!" Akash exclaimed with a baffled look.

"It is also newly built." Nitya said. "We can visit it when everyone of us is there."

"Okay." Dhruv said. "So, shall we move on?"

"Yes." Everyone else said. They paid their bill and moved towards their homes.

After having his dinner, Akash straight away walked towards his bedroom. While lying on the bed and staring on the ceiling, he was just wondering about the whole day. He was happy after a long time and was eagerly waiting for his upcoming days when all his friends would be with him. Then, his mobile phone made a 'beep' sound. He saw that Nitya had uploaded their photos on their whatsapp group. He downloaded the photos which gave a hint of a smile on his face. Then, he kept his mobile phone on his bedside table and went to sleep.

After two days, when Akash was about to sit for his breakfast, the doorbell rang. Pratima opened the door and saw Rohan outside. "Hey, what a surprise!" Pratima said.

"Good morning Aunty. Is Akash there?" Rohan asked. Akash heard his voice and so, he immediately ran towards the entrance. "Hey, what a pleasant surprise!" Akash said as he was happily startled to see Rohan over there. Rohan had reached Dhran in the morning. They had planned to have Misal-pav for breakfast and so, he visited Akash to inform about the same.

"Oh! Wait. I am coming." Akash said and immediately went inside to get his scooter's key. But seeing him in a hurry, Pratima again reminded him about his studies.

"I will do it maa." Akash said and excitedly went out.

"Let it be Pratima. Let him enjoy these days. After a huge time, we are seeing our son happy and excited." Prashant said as he and Pratima saw their son joining his friends.

Akash was too excited to meet his childhood friends. He even met Ankita over there. Then, they moved towards Jalaram restaurant to have Misal-pav.

Soon, they had reached Jalaram restaurant. It was the most famous spot in the town for having Misal-pav. They booked their table and ordered Misal-pav for everyone.

"It's been so long I have had Misal-pav." Ankita said.

"You must be getting it in Indore, don't you?" Nitya asked.

"Yeah, but I haven't tried much. I used to have Poha over there." Ankita said.

"You shameless, you should have brought some Poha over here." Akash japed.

"You should have come to Indore to have it." Ankita said jokingly as the Misal-pav plates arrived. They again took the pictures and started having the dish. They were enjoying the Misal-pav a lot. Meanwhile, they even decided to go for trekking at Inglal fort the next day.

Then, soon they had finished having their breakfast. "Does anyone want more, or shall we move?" Akash asked.

"We will move." Ankita said and so, everyone agreed. They paid the bill at the counter and moved out. They again took a group photo outside the restaurant and then uploaded all the pictures on their whatsapp group. Then, after reaching their colony, they played badminton and other games, recreating their childhood memories.

Then the evening, they had again visited Khau-galli. They again went to stall number thirteen and ordered Soya bean Chilli and Paneer Chilli. Then, as they were chattering, suddenly Rohan's mobile phone rang. "Yeah, we have reached." He said on his phone and cut the call. Then he saw everyone glaring at him.

"Who is coming?" Akash asked in astonishment. So Rohan looked at everyone nervously and said, "Ah! Guys, actually I want to tell you something. There is someone who is coming to meet us." A total silence spread. Then, Ankita asked, "Who is she?" as she had got a hint that Rohan is having a girlfriend.

"Actually she is Manisha, my girlfriend." Rohan said.

"You scoundrel! You are having a girlfriend and you are making us aware now." Nitya scolded Rohan in a friendly way.

"Actually I wanted to surprise you all." Rohan tried to explain.

"So, today Rohan is giving us a treat." Dhruv japed. But Akash was shocked to know about Rohan's relationship. He had not expected anyone from his group to have a love-affair. Forget about girlfriend, he did not even had a good friend in his college. But still he was happy for Rohan.

Then everyone saw two girls coming towards them. They were Manisha and her friend Sonakshi, as Rohan introduced.

"Hello everyone." Manisha said. So, everyone wished both of them back. They both had their seats next to Rohan.

"Couldn't you find some better guy then this idiot?" Nitya japed at Manisha.

"I could have, but he is cute." Manisha said and so everyone teased Rohan, "Ohooooo." Then, the waiter brought the dishes. But as he placed one of the dishes near Rohan, Akash pulled the dish by saying in a playful manner, "You are not supposed to eat alone." But immediately he saw Sonakshi pulling her hand back as she was about to grab a piece from that plate. So, Akash placed the plate back near her and said, "Oh! I am sorry. I didn't see you." Everyone had a laugh on that incident.

Akash's friends had a great talk with Manisha and Sonakshi. Manisha told them that she knew Rohan since their first year in the college, but proposed him when they had gone to Kullu-Manali for college trip last year.

"You proposed him!" Nitya was startled. "How can you propose someone who looks like a gorilla?" Everyone had a guffaw at her joke.

"What the hell was that?" Rohan was startled to hear that, but everyone just continued laughing. While continuing their talks, they even asked Manisha and Sonakshi to join them for Inglal fort trekking the next day. Then soon, they had completed the meal. They paid off the bill, took group photos, and moved towards the pedestrian bridge. As they reached the bridge, they parked their vehicles at the river bank and climbed it.

"Wow." Akash said as he was overwhelmed by the river view from its top.

"The river looks so beautiful from here." Minakshi said. They even took photographs over there, had cotton candies and did all sorts of crazy things. Akash had finally started enjoying. He had started living the way he wanted. Though his time didn't rewind, he still got what he had wished for.

"Guys, now let us leave. Early morning we have to leave." Ankita said and so everyone agreed to her and started leaving. "Everyone please upload the pics on whatsapp group."

Everyone had reached home. Before going to bed, Akash was going through all his pictures in his mobile phone. He was enjoying the moment so much that he had forgotten all his college tension. Then, he sat the alarm of 5 A.M. and went to sleep as next morning they had planned a track to Inglal fort.

Next morning, as Akash was about to move out of the house to call his friends, the doorbell rang. He realised that his friends would have come to call him. He furtively wore his jacket, hand gloves and a woolen cap and went to the door to open it. But as he opened it, he was terribly startled. None of his friends were at the entrance.

"Surprise!" Tejas said as he had reached there.

"Tejas!" Akash was shocked to see him. Even Pratima and Prashant came out to see him.

"You should have informed us." Prashant said.

"I wanted to surprise you all." Tejas said while touching his parents' feet.

"Now go inside and have some rest." Pratima said.

"No, you come with us. We are going to Inglal fort." Akash said.

"Okay, so let us inform Dhaval, Sejal and Manish." Tejas said.

"Dhaval, Sejal and Manish!" Akash said as he was again shocked to hear their names. "Are they here?"

"Akash." Akash heard Dhaval's call from outside. He saw Dhaval, Sejal, Minakshi, Nitya, Dhruv and Rohan waiting outside to leave. Akash excitedly ran out along with Tejas to meet them. Everyone was wearing jacket, hand gloves and woolen caps as it was extreme cold.

"You Rascals. You all didn't even call us." Akash said in a playful manner to Dhaval, Sejal and Manish. He was shivering. Then, everyone saw Manisha and Sonakshi coming towards them. Rohan introduced them to Dhaval, Sejal, Manish and Tejas as they gave a baffled look at both of them.

"Manisha is 'will-be Mrs. Rohan'." Nitya clarified and so, Manisha again had a blush.

"Oh! That's nice." Dhaval said as he was a bit shocked. Then, again he added, "Guys, Ankita will join us at Sardar Patel chowk. We are supposed to wait for her over there."

"But why?" Dhruv asked as everyone was bemused.

"Guys, can we discuss this afterwards. We are supposed to reach Inglal fort before the dawn." Dhaval said. So, they rode towards Sardar Patel chowk. But as they reached, they saw Ankita reaching towards them. But wait, they were seeing a girl with her. Everyone felt silent, wondering who she was. So, to break the silence, Dhaval said, "Guys, this is Prajakta."

"Will-be Mrs. Dhaval." Ankita added. Everyone was shocked to know that even Dhaval was engaged.

"Oh! So, we having one more guy who has fallen prey." Nitya said. Everyone was amazed to know about Prajakta.

"What the hell is all going on? All the gorillas and donkeys are having girlfriends and we humans are still single." Dhruv japed. And so, everyone had a guffaw while Dhaval and Rohan stared at him.

Then, they had started moving. It was too cold and everyone was shivering throughout the way. Soon they had reached Inglal fort which was on the highway. The Inglal fort was a mountain fort. So, they had to park their vehicles at the mountain's base and then climb the mountain.

"Does anyone know the history of this fort?" Ankita asked while climbing.

"This fort was made around fourteenth century by Farooqi Empire when they were ruling over Khandesh." Akash said.

"Fourteenth century! This fort is seven hundred years old!" Sonakshi said as she was shocked to hear that.

"Yes." Akash replied.

"By the way, Manisha, Sonakshi and Prajakta, this is Akash – the walking history book of our group. If you want to know anything regarding Indian history then just ask him." Rohan said. "But I didn't get one thing. How come Prajakta was with Ankita?"

"Dhaval had told me about Prajakta some days back. He even told me that she was coming to Dhran along with him. But, it was not preferable for her to stay at Dhaval's place. So, Dhaval had told me to take her to my place." Ankita said.

"And my parents are not aware about her, just mind that." Dhaval warned everyone. "Even if they see her along with us, she is just Ankita's friend to them. Is that okay?"

"No, that is not at all okay." Rohan teased Dhaval. "You can't cheat your parents. I will definitely tell them that they are having a daughter-in-law."

"Before you do that shit, I will throw you down from this fort and let Manisha get widowed before your marriage." Dhaval warned Rohan in a playful manner.

"Oh! Is it?" Rohan asked in a playful way. "Come on, we still have a long way to climb." So, they again started climbing. While moving towards the top, they had started taking heavy breaths.

"Can we-halt-for sometime?" Minakshi asked with heavy breaths. She saw a huge rock and immediately sat on it.

"No.   The-more-we-stop-the-more-we-will-get-tired." Tejas said while taking heavy breaths. He wanted to tell that they lacked time as they would miss sunrise but he didn't have energy for extra words. They all continued moving while helping each other.

Soon, they had reached a huge dry well which had a structure with a dome roof near it. Both the well and the structure were in ruins. They waited for a while over there while still taking heavy breaths. "What is this?" Nitya asked.

"The kings and the queens used to bathe in the well and then dry themselves and wear clothes in this broken structure." Rohan jested.

"Yeah, this chap was there at that time to see them bathing." Ankita jested too.

"Wow! What a view it is." Manisha exclaimed seeing the view below. But they even got the hint of the sunlight at far end towards the east. So, they again started climbing. The more they were climbing, the more they were getting tired.

The mountain looked easy to climb from the bottom, but it wasn't. Soon they had neared the fort. But as they reached the top, they couldn't find the entrance. They were totally exhausted. But the sweat and cool breeze was making them feel better. It seemed they were on the wrong path. They couldn't find the entrance. But still they continued moving.

Soon, Tejas shouted, "I have found it. Here it is." They had found the entrance. But there was no way seen towards it. It seemed to be the thief-gate, but they were still discussing how they were supposed to climb. Then, they saw some steep steps carved out of stones which were leading towards the door.

"Please someone tell me that these are not the steps." Akash said as he was shocked to see those steep steps.

"No, this seems the only way up." Dhaval said and started climbing. "Be careful everyone." He warned as everyone followed him. The steps were slippery to climb. They had to hook to their fingers to the above steps for support. Akash was too nervous to climb. But as he saw everyone else, he gathered self-confidence within himself and managed to climb.

"Woohoo! What a view." Tejas said as they saw the sunrise at far end. The view from the top was amazing. It was too cold on the top. Everyone was shivering. The sunrise was beautiful from the top. They all enjoyed the view from the top.

"It seems that no one is taking care of this fort." Akash said as they saw some of the walls in ruined state.

"May be its difficult to get repairing material upto this height. There is no proper access." Dhaval said.

They were roaming throughout the fort. But most of the fort was in dilapidated condition. "Where is the main entrance?" Dhruv asked.

"May be it must have been within one of these broken walls in the past." Prajakta said.

Akash and his friends enjoyed for a couple of hours over there. As usual, they took pictures of the surrounding and themselves. Even Dhaval-Prajakta and Rohan-Manisha were busy taking pictures of themselves together. Akash felt that they were so lucky, as they had a partner to love them.

The sun had risen completely. The fort was so small that they were done within a couple of hours. Then, they decided to climb down. But as they reached the door through which they had entered, a challenge befell upon them – the steep steps. Now, how are they supposed to climb down, they discussed. They started climbing down one person at a time. Rohan was the first one to dare.

The space for placing the foot was too narrow, making it difficult for the climbers. Rohan had to face his chest towards the steps while climbing down slowly and steadily while hooking his fingers on the upper steps. But somehow, he managed. He gave a *thumb's up* sign to everyone above as he reached down, signaling them to climb down.

Akash was getting nervous. He was just standing behind, letting everyone pass first. Then, it was his turn. On seeing the depth he needed to climb, his heart was pounding heavily. He wasn't able to gather confidence.

"Akash, what happened?" Manish asked on seeing his bemused face. "Come on, you can do it."

Akash's fear was making it more difficult than it really was. So, he took a deep breath, gathered confidence, and started climbing down. He was much slower than the others for climbing down. The dew was making the steps much slippery. Then, finally he reached down. And took a sigh of relief.

"Akash, you need to be a daredevil." Dhaval said. Then, soon they reached down the hill.

Everyone was hungry by the time they had reached the foot of the hill. So, again they decided to have Misal-pav at Jalaram restaurant. Soon, they furtively rode towards Jalaram restaurant. Over there, they had joined two tables so they all could sit together. They ordered each plate for everyone.

Everyone was tired out of the trek, with their hands and legs throbbing. But still they enjoyed a lot. Then immediately, their plates arrived and they had their breakfast. They even took pictures over there and forwarded to everyone on their whatsapp group.

Everyone had spent their day very well. They had even planned lunch and dinner at the new food outlets which had recently started in Jay nagar. And for the next day, they had planned to visit a famous tea stall – Kajal's tea point in the morning and then go to Korabod tekdi.

Next morning, everyone had gathered again by 5 A.M. and straight away went to Kajal's tea point. But as they reached over there, they saw that it wasn't that crowded as it would be after eight o'clock. It was the most famous tea point in the town. They parked their scooters, went to the counter and ordered the tea for everyone. Soon, the waiter brought the tea in the tray and they all had it.

What was liked the most about the tea point was its antique cup-saucers. Everyone enjoyed a lot to have sips from the saucers. They all took pictures of themselves and even the cup-saucers and uploaded on their whatsapp group. After they were done, they moved towards Korabod tekdi.

The Korabod tekdi was ahead of Inglal fort on the same highway. It was a hill where a famous Maratha era temple was. They parked their vehicles at the hill's foot and started climbing till the top.

"Akash, do you know the history of this temple?" Manisha asked.

"Yes, of course." Akash replied excitedly. "This temple is around two hundred and fifty years old. The Marathas had built this after capturing the Inglal fort from the Mughals in the year 1760."

"How come do you know all this?" Manish asked.

"I love Indian history." Akash said. Then they visited the temple.

Everyone was enjoying a lot on the hill. They stayed over there for a couple of hours and took pictures over there.

At the day's end, Akash was going through all his pictures with his friends which gave a smile on his face. He was seeing this beautiful days for the first time in his college life.

CHAPTER FIVE

Akash was spending his days with his friends very well. He had even uploaded all his photos on his Facebook profile page. So, all his college mates would like it and give good comments. He was feeling very happy on seeing people respond to his happy memories.

Then, the 31st of December arrived. Akash and his friends had planned a New Year party on Ankita's terrace. They spend the whole day buying the decoration materials. They had very well decorated the terrace. After the sunset, they had planned to gather at Ankita's place.

While Akash was getting ready for the New Year party, he heard a knock on his door. He saw it was Pratima. "Yes, maa." Akash said nervously as Pratima glared at him.

"Tonight should be your last to enjoy. From tomorrow, I want you back with your studies." Pratima warned as Akash still had four subjects to clear.

"Yes, maa." Akash replied. Afterwards, he went out along with Tejas to join his friends.

All of Akash's friends had reached Ankita's place. They straight away went to the terrace to start the party. They had decorated the terrace by themselves. Though it was simple but it was elegant. The whole parapet wall was decorated with lightings. Snack and dinner items were arranged on the tables in one corner and seating mats were placed throughout the terrace. As everyone sat on the mats,

Dhaval asked, they started making a list of what they could play as they still had four hours for the mid-night.

"Can we play eating-eating?" Rohan japed. "And where are the disco lights?"

"Next year you sponsor us and we will have everything you want." Nitya said jokingly.

"Oh! Is it? But I am completely fine with this." Rohan said in a playful way. Then, they started playing all the games. They were enjoying the moment very much. They did all the crazy stuff and not to forget, they took photographs of each and every moment. Even Dhaval-Prajakta and Rohan-Manisha made their couple photo-shoot. Then, only a couple of minutes were remaining for twelve O'clock.

"Guys, it's almost time. Let's ready the cake." Dhruv said. So, they brought the table to the center and placed the cake on it, and waited for midnight.

"Guys, only a few seconds are remaining." Akash said. "Five-four-three-two-one-zero."

"HAPPY NEW YEAR." Everyone shouted happily and cut the cake.

"HAPPY NEW YEAR." They all wished everyone and shared the cake bites. They even saw the crackers bursting in the sky by some other people at far ends. Then, soon they had their dinner. Even, while having dinner they had all sorts of fun and took pictures.

"Now what is the plan for tomorrow?" Akash asked excitedly.

"Returning back to the pavilion." Dhruv said.

"Oh!" Akash said in a low voice. Akash realised that soon his friends would be returning back and his happy days would get over. Their colleges were starting. They would really miss those days but not more than Akash.

They continued their talks and having laughs except for Akash. He was in his pensive, worrying about his college days. Then, as they were done, they wrapped and placed everything on their respective places. After ending everything, they said good bye to everyone with a heavy heart and went home.

While lying on the bed, Akash was just wondering about those happy days of him which would never return. Tejas was fast asleep. So, he allowed his tears to roll out of his eyes and tip on his pillow. Then, he wiped his eyes and went to sleep.

Next morning, as Akash woke up, he saw his whatsapp flooded with messages of 'Happy new year.' But he avoided every group and clicked on his friends' group and saw that everyone had uploaded their pictures and videos. He too shared the pictures and videos from his phone. Then, he saved all the pictures and videos in his computer and uploaded on his Facebook profile page. He was very happy seeing those pictures and videos, but he knew that those days had ended. That made him sad.

"Akash, first have your breakfast and then do all this stuff." Pratima said while standing at his room's entrance.

"Just give me a couple of minutes, maa." Akash said with a heavy heart. After he was done, he brushed his teeth and went down to have his breakfast. Akash saw that Prashant was watching the television while Tejas had already started having his breakfast. Then, Pratima passed the plate of Poha towards Akash. But, as Akash started eating, he heard an advertisement on the television. It was a telecom company's advertisement highlighting the bond between friends through mobile phones. The title of the advertisement's song was – *each and every friend is important.*

Each and every friend is important – this line rang inside Akash's mind. Then, an idea clicked in his mind. He furtively finished his breakfast and ran towards his room.

"What happened?" Tejas asked but Akash couldn't reply. Prashant and Pratima just looked on. Akash entered his room in a hurry, took a pen and a book and started noting down all the moments which he had spent with his friends. He noted everything regarding the places they had visited and all sort of stuff they had done according to the dates. Then, he started writing down a poem on his friends on the same tune as that of the advertisement's song.

Each and every friend is important – he gave this line as the title of the poem. He described all his precious moments in that poem and gave the tune as that of the song. Then, after a couple of hours, he completed the poem and took his book to his friend.

Akash called all his friends outside. "What happened?" They asked as they were lacking time to pack their luggage. They all had gathered on one spot.

"Guys, I have a surprise for you all." Akash said.

"What surprise?" Manish asked. So, Akash opened his book and started reading his poem. He was reading it in the same tune as that of the song. And then, he finished.

Everyone was astonished to hear that poem from Akash.

"Is this written by you?" Ankita asked in amazement.

"Yeah, how's it?" Akash asked.

"It's awesome, speechless." Manish said in excitement.

"I can't believe this is written by you." Dhaval said amazement.

"Even I didn't know that my brother is such a good writer." Tejas said. Akash felt happy listening to their comments.

"Akash, you have very well elaborated what we all have experienced these days." Minakshi said.

"So guys, now we are having a writer in our group." Rohan said.

"Akash, can you sent us a PDF of this poem on whatsapp?" Nitya asked.

"Yeah, we can have it as a memory of these days." Sejal said.

"But how am I supposed to make a PDF file?" Akash asked as he lacked knowledge about computer software.

"Don't worry, it's an engineer's job, not a writer's job. I will do it for you. And it's not 'PDF file'. It's just PDF. The 'F' itself stands for 'File'." Rohan said. He took the pictures of the poem with his mobile phone's camera.

"Guys, we should leave now. We still have to do packing." Ankita said. "Akash, you do post your poem on our Facebook page. You are a writer now." She added. Then, everyone moved towards their home.

Akash was deeply moved that day. He was in his room, trying to study. But Tejas' line 'Even I didn't know that my brother is such a good writer', Rohan's line 'So, now we are having a writer in our group' and Ankita's line 'You are a writer now' was running inside his mind. No one had praised him so much like that till then. He was a writer. He had realised that he had the quality of writing inside him.

Akash had realised that he was good in writing. But soon, he realised that he had exams after two months. So, he continued with his studies. Everyday, while studying, he would take a break and read his poem secretly. But he was aware of the fact that his poem was not going to help him in his exams. So, he tried his level best to concentrate on his studies.

During his exams in Pune, he had stayed at Janhvi's house. As earlier, he would go to his college, see his classmates in senior class and get hurt, appear for the exams and return back. This happened throughout the exams. Akash knew that his exams were not good, but still he would pretend in front in front of his parents that he would pass.

It was the last day of Akash's exams. Janhvi asked him about his exams in an amiable way as he returned home.

"Good, as usual." Akash replied while removing his shoes in the lobby.

"Good? Or as usual?" Janhvi japed. Akash realised what she meant and so, both of them had a guffaw.

Then, after the lunch, as Akash was moving inside, his eyes befell on a set of D.V.D.s on the television's shelf. Akash took those DVDs in his hands to see what movies it had. Those were the different parts of '*The lord of the rings*' movies' set. Janhvi realised that he was interested in those movies. "I even have novels of these series. Take these D.V.D.s and the novels with you and return it to me once you come back to Pune." Janhvi said.

"Thank you aunty." Akash said with a radiant smile.

"But be careful. These are my precious." Janhvi jested.

Akash happily took the books and the D.V.D.s along with him. Then, he went inside to pack his luggage as he had to leave for Dhran in the evening.

After reaching Dhran the next day, the first thing Akash did was to watch those movies. Akash was very much fond of medieval period. So, he found those movies very interesting. He spent his whole day watching those movies.

Some of Akash's friends had got placements in various companies and some were preparing for post-graduation. Tejas' exams were still going on. So, he was all alone. For a couple of days, he would just watch other movies and read his poem which he had written for his friends. But he didn't want to be a poet. Once he was in his room and was glaring at the novels which Janhvi had given to him. He was wondering how the writer imagined that fiction-fantasy story, wrote it down and published it to the masses.

"Did you like the novel?" Pratima asked as she entered his room. She was noticing Akash concentrating on the novels and the movies since last two days.

"Oh! Maa." Akash was surprised. He kept the novels on the side.

"Is there anything you want to share, son?" Pratima asked politely. "I am your mother. You can share it with me."

"Nothing such." Akash quavered.

"Anyways, you are developing a new hobby of reading. Janhvi told me about the novels and the movies she gave it to you. It's really good." Pratima said.

"Thanks maa." Akash said. Then, Pratima kissed his forehead and left the room. Akash again took the novels and started reading the first part. But as he turned a couple of pages, an idea clicked in him. He asked himself that why is he not writing a story of that same genre. He loved history. So, he thought that he should write a story set in medieval period. He got an idea of a fiction-fantasy story completely written by him.

Akash knew that he was interested only in history. So, he decided to develop a fiction-fantasy story set in the medieval age. He straight away went down to his parents' room and took one of the new diaries of his father. Prashant was an oil paint dealer and on every New Year, he would receive diaries as a gift from the oil paint companies of whose dealership he had. Akash read the company's name on the cover page with the message of 'Happy New Year 2012'. Then, he took the diary to his room.

Akash readied his study table, adjusted his chair, opened his new diary, took his pen, gathered some ideas and directly started writing down his new book. He would write down all the sentences and scenes which would come into his mind.

Akash spend his whole day writing his story. Next early morning, the doorbell rang. Prashant and Pratima opened the door and saw that Tejas was back home. He happily touched his parents' feet and carried his luggage up to his bedroom. But, though he entered his room cautiously, Akash woke up. "Hey, when did you come?" Akash asked.

"Just now. How are you?" Tejas asked.

"I am fine. What about you?" Akash asked.

"I am good too." Tejas said. Then he opened his suitcase and took out some books and passed it to Akash. "This is for you. The song of ice and fire series. Maa told me yesterday that you have started reading these type of books. So, I bought this for you."

"Is this having stories of kings and emperors?" Akash asked.

"It's not a real story but you will like the politics, wars and what all it has." Tejas said. "And this pen drive has movie series of it." Tejas added while passing the pen drive to Akash.

"Oh! Thanks a lot." Akash said excitedly. He straight away switched on his computer, attached Tejas' pen drive to it and started watching the movie.

"Bhaiya, at least have your breakfast first. And why are you watching the movie before reading the book? You will lose the fun." Tejas said.

"But what difference does it make? The story is the same, isn't it?" Akash asked.

"No. The book is the real story. But for making a movie, they have to cut or edit some scenes." Tejas said.

"Oh!" Akash said. Then he shut down the computer, got ready and went down to have his breakfast. Prashant was already off to his shop. Pratima was cooking food in the kitchen and only Tejas was there along with Akash on the dining table. Akash wanted to tell his family that he was planning to write a novel. But he couldn't do it. His words had reached his tongue, but he didn't have courage and confidence to let it out. So, he just thought of first completing his book and then let his family know about it. But after the breakfast, as Akash went to his room and continued with his writing, Tejas came and saw him with his book. "What are you writing?" He asked eagerly.

"Ah!" Akash hesitated. He had to reveal what was he upto as Tejas had caught him. He paused for a second and continued, "I am writing a book."

"Oh! Wow. You are writing a book! Show me." Tejas said excitedly.

"Actually I have just begun." Akash said nervously.

"But what is the genre?" Tejas asked.

"Genre? What does that mean?" Akash asked dumbly.

"Genre means, whether it is a thriller, or suspense, or comedy, or fiction, or fantasy, or historic, or romantic, or whatever." Tejas said.

"It is like the ones which you and Janhvi aunty gave to me." Akash said.

"Okay, that means it's a fiction-fantasy book." Tejas said. "So, you should definitely first read the books. You will get to know how the author has described the scenes and the characters, how the plot is made, the grammar, the communication between the characters, and much more. The reader should get the same picture in front of him as that of the one in the writer's mind. That's the trick. First, you learn all this and then write."

"Okay." Akash said in an agreeing manner. He understood what Tejas said. So, he immediately kept his book on the side and took the first book of *The song of ice and fire* and started reading it.

It was for the first time that Akash was reading a book. He straight away went to the main content to know the story. But, as he finished a couple of pages, he found it a bit difficult to understand. He found words that he was reading for the first time. So, he had to take his dictionary to understand the meaning.

Akash was reading the novel and side-by-side surfing the dictionary. But that seemed a bit irritating to him. He was losing the link to the story. Then, during the lunch time, Tejas revealed to Pratima that Akash was writing a fiction-fantasy novel.

"What novel?" Pratima asked Akash in astonishment. Akash looked at her nervously and replied, "Actually it's like the one which Janhvi aunty Tejas has given to me. What I am writing is a story of an emperor whose prince is the hero and there is a villain with some supernatural powers."

"Why are you being so nervous while telling this?" Pratima asked but Akash couldn't reply. "Be confident. You won't be able to make others believe your story unless and until you are confident about it."

"But bhaiya, your story doesn't seem unique. That's why I am telling you to first read the novels, and learn from them how a good story is made. And only after completing those novels, you start writing your own book." Tejas said.

"Okay." Akash agreed. "But there is a problem. The language and wording are too difficult. By the time I find the meaning from the dictionary, I lose the link."

"You can do one thing. Take another diary of your father and divide it alphabet-wise. And note down those difficult words with their meanings in their alphabet columns. Through this, you will learn new words which can be useful in your book too." Pratima said.

So, after the lunch, Akash took another diary of Prashant, went to his room, and divided it alphabet wise. Then, again he started reading the novel from the beginning.

While Akash was reading the first novel, he again came across the same difficult words. So, he started noting them down with their meanings in his new diary. Then again he would read the sentence keeping the meaning in mind, to get a better understanding. Many a times, he would encounter sentences which had a simple meaning but were written in such a polished language that it would impress the readers.

Akash had fallen in love with that novel. He was deeply moved by the way the author had written it. He would sit with that novel all day till he completed. It took him a couple of weeks to complete the novel including writing down the difficult words. He had got used to those difficult words so much that even if he encountered them again, he didn't had to find the meaning. He had learned most of the words' meanings by heart.

Soon, Akash's one-and-a-half months' vacation was about to end. By then, he had already completed reading three books. For the second and third book, he didn't had to note down much of the difficult words. Much of the words were getting repeated and he had learned their meanings by heart.

Akash was too upset to return back to Pune even though he was promoted to fourth year. His mind was completed diverted from architecture to writing. He was so engrossed in writing that he had completely forgotten about his college days. He had started enjoying his days so much that he didn't want his time to rewind as he wished earlier. He was half-heartedly packing his suitcase. While he was packing, Pratima entered his room. "You are upset, aren't you?" Pratima asked.

"No maa. Why do you think so?" Akash asked.

"Because I am your mother and I can read your emotions." Pratima said. "By the way, how many books did you finish?"

"Three." Akash said.

"Oh! That's great. So my boy is developing a passion." Pratima said in a motivational way. Then, she saw Akash keeping the novels and his diaries in his luggage. "Akash, you should not take this with you. This will distract you from your studies." She tried to stop him.

"Maa please. Let me take it." Akash tried to persuade her.

"No Akash. You have already lost one year. I don't want you to divert your mind in your fourth year." Pratima warned. So, Akash halfheartedly removed his books from his suitcase, kept it back in his cupboard and went on with his luggage packing.

"All the best my boy." Pratima said while kissing Akash's forehead. Then, she left the room. So, taking the golden chance, Akash took back his books and kept it in his suitcase.

Akash had to leave for Pune to attend his college. Prashant had done his admission in the same hostel as earlier. Tejas had already left for Mumbai a couple of days back. But before leaving, Prashant handed him. "It's a laptop computer for you." He said.

"Laptop computer!" Akash was startled. Even Pratima gave a bewilder look. "But there isn't any need for this."

"This is the problem with you. You never know what is all going on around you regarding you." Prashant taunted him. "In your fourth year and fifth year, you will require this to use AutoCAD. It's a software for making architectural drawings." Prashant said. Akash felt a bit shy because of his absentmindedness. "Thank you papa." He said happily. Then, as he was getting late, he immediately kept his computer in his suitcase. Then, he touched his parents' feet and then Prashant took him to the bus stop on his scooter. Pratima had a doubt that Akash would have taken his books along. So, after they were gone, she went to Akash's room to search his cupboard. But even after a prolong search, she couldn't find the books. Her doubt was true. And now she was afraid that Akash was planning to divert his mind from architecture to writing.

CHAPTER SIX

Akash had reached Pune the next day. As usual, Amit had reached to receive him. "Welcome back." Amit greeted him.

While they both were on their way towards their hostel, they had a good talk as they were meeting after almost a year. When Amit asked him about his holidays, Akash told him that he spent his time reading the novels given by Tejas. He even told him that he had the movies with him.

"Oh! Those are amazing series." Amit said. Then, they had reached the hostel. Akash had got another room this time. His previous room, which he shared with Amit, Sahil and Rishabh was already occupied by some other tenant. But still, his room was on the same floor as that of his.

Akash had reached his new room. His new room-mates were Rakesh, Ritesh and Kushal. He knew them since his first year at college. They were good friends and so, he didn't had to worry. Then, as Akash occupies his bed, his phone rang. He saw that it was Pratima's call. "Hello maa." He said.

"Have you reached?" Pratima asked.

"Yeah, just now I reached." Akash said.

"Okay, and where are your books?" Pratima asked but Akash hesitated to answer.

"It's...... in my cupboard." Akash replied hesitantly.

"Akash, don't lie to me. I have searched every corner of your room." Pratima said while Prashant was listening.

"It's with me, maa." Akash said with a guilty voice.

"Akash, I had refrained you. Why are you doing this?" Pratima asked but Akash couldn't answer. Her anger was crossing limits. She seemed very upset. "Answer me Akash."

"Maa don't worry. I will do my studies." Akash said. Then, Pratima paused for a second, took a deep breath and said, "I don't want complaints from your class teacher this year. Is that understood?"

"Yes maa. Bye." Akash said and ended the call.

Prashant asked Pratima about the matter. So, she revealed everything about his book.

"Pratima, just relax. That won't happen." Prashant said while trying to comfort her.

"Hope so." Pratima said. Then they both went to the dining hall to have their breakfast.

In Pune, even Akash had his breakfast and was about to leave for his college. He had to take the intracity bus to reach his college as he didn't have his bike that day. And unlike last time, he had taken only one note book along with him. He had reached his college before time as usual. He was worried, thinking about his new classmates. Who would befriend him and who would not, he didn't know. He waited at the building's entrance as it was still closed. Then, the other students started reaching over there. Some of them were his juniors, some of them were his present classmates and some of them were his ex-classmates who were now in fifth year. He was again hurt seeing his old classmates, but he avoided them as they wouldn't bother to even look at him. Even though he still had some of his old class-mates along with him who had failed too, still he felt bad for himself. But he had to continue what life had placed before him. "I wish I could rewind the time." He said in his heart to himself to be with his childhood friends for one last time and enjoy those moments.

Akash had made up his mind to give his best in his in his fourth year. But he also knew that every year he would encourage himself on the first day, but nothing worked. On the first day, he was with his previous class-mates as the class was completely new to him.

The first day of his college just had introduction to the subjects. After the college, he straight away went to the transported to get his scooter. After that, he reached his hostel, had his lunch and immediately went to his room to call Pratima. Both mother and son had a good talk, and again Pratima reminded him about not to use his books during his studies. Akash had assured her that he would keep his words, but still Pratima had a doubt on him.

Then, after the call, he took the pen-drive which Tejas had given to him and unboxed his new laptop computer. He was very excited seeing his new computer. Then, he inserted the pen-drive in it and started watching the movies. Tejas had warned him to read the books before the movies, but he couldn't resist. He had ample of time on his first day. Even he was worried that he had to return the D.V.D.s and the novels to Janhvi as soon as possible. He liked those movies so much that even on the Sundays, he would watch it along with Amit.

The days went on. Akash's workload was going on increasing. This time he had to do more case studies, presentation work, and all other stuff than his previous years. He tried his level best to cope up, but still ended being nothing. The worst part was, his link was completely broken due to his one year gap. So. His situation was getting from bad to worst.

Akash was very much addicted to novel reading. Whenever he would get time, he would read it, especially on weekends. But for his college submissions, his mind would get chocked up. He wouldn't get any idea to carry forwards his designs. Forget about out of the box, his designs were not even architecturally workable. So, for every jury presentation, his work was always one of the worst. So, prior to his first semester exams, again Pratima had received a call from Professor Kajal Kadam. She had the same complain against Akash as that of his previous years regarding his performance.

After the meeting, Pratima was very much frustrated. She had called Akash at Janhvi's place. "What the hell is all going on Akash?" She asked angrily. "Are you really interested in this field or not?"

"Yes maa, I am interested." Akash said dumbly.

"Yeah, I can see." Pratima said. "During your holidays, you were applying your full efforts behind your book. You should give that same amount of efforts for your studies too. And again I am warning you, don't divert your mind now. This is not the right time."

"Yeah maa, I know." Akash said.

"Have you brought those novels?" Pratima asked.

"Yeah." Akash said. Then, with a heavy heart, he took out the novels from his bag and handed them to her. Those novels were given to him by Janhvi and Tejas. He didn't want to do that. He was feeling like he was giving out his heart. Even Pratima felt that she was taking away something precious from his son. He had also brought the D.V.D.s which he handed back to Janhvi.

The days went on. Then, Akash's exams were declared. But he couldn't complete his housing project from architectural design. So, he was told by his professor Kajal

Kadam to complete it in his vacation after the first semester exams.

During his vacation, Akash would visit his college to discuss his design with his professor. Not only him, but few of his classmates who were failing in the subject would visit the college for their design discussion. Akash's whole vacation was spend behind the housing design. Then, at the end of the vacation, he was able to submit his housing project.

Akash's second semester had started. But at the same time, even his result was declared. He was failing in three major subjects. He was hesitant to call his parents, but still he had to herald them.

"What is all going on Akash?" Prashant asked in astonishment. But Akash couldn't reply. "Don't be quiet. I am asking you."

"Yes papa, I am listening." Akash said in a guilty voice.

"Don't just listen, do something." Prashant persuaded. "Akash, I just want to tell you one thing. If it's not happening then, let us know. We have a business over here and you can handle it. I am not discouraging you but just giving you an option."

"No papa, I can continue." Akash said even though he was confused whether he would be firm on his words or not.

"Think and decide. Your whole career depends on your decision. You take one wrong step and everything will be over." Prashant said.

After the call, Akash was completely perturbed, emotionally and mentally. The more he tried, the more he was losing interest in the course. Just like his previous classes, he would miss all the deadlines and remain behind his classmates. Just like his previous classes, he had become a joke in this class too.

Akash's second semester was same as that of first. He had come to know that Shreyas and his other old classmates had started their internship at some architectural firms. They were getting paid, while he was here, still struggling to cope up with his assignment. He wasn't able to handle the mental strain on himself. So, one day he made a call to Prashant.

"Papa......... actually I am not able to continue." Akash said. He was hesitating while talking.

"What do you mean, son?" Prashant asked to clarify.

"Can I came back to Dhran.......... and handle your business?" Akash asked in a pleading voice. He was about to cry.

"You are talking like a looser, son." Prashant said. But Akash couldn't answer. "I know it's getting tough for you. But there must be some way out." Prashant tried to encourage him. "Son, think twice before giving up and then decide. You still have time till your exams."

"Papa please." Akash persuaded. "I don't want to stay here anymore."

"No Akash, you are not coming back without giving your exams. Is that clear? I am not saying that you have to pass, but at least you can try." Prashant said. "I will accept you as a failure after giving the exams. But I will not accept you as a coward who runs away from it. Be brave and face your difficulties."

Prashant was very much upset the whole day after talking to Akash. He was afraid since his son's first year that he had done a mistake by admitting Akash in Architecture. Even Pratima knew that their son was developing interest in writing. Their fear had proven true.

In the evening, when Prashant had returned home, Pratima saw him upset. "What happened?" She asked him.

"Today Akash had called me." Prashant said while sitting on the sofa. "He wants to leave architecture and come back."

"What!" Pratima was startled to hear that. She had a doubt that her son was diverting his mind, and her doubt was proving true. "Then, what did you say?"

"I have warned him that he has to appear for the exams. But I guess he has made up his mind for giving up his studies." Prashant said.

"Let me talk to him." Pratima said and went inside to get her mobile phone.

"Just talk to him and don't scold him. He is already under pressure." Prashant said as Pratima was searching Akash's name in her contact list.

"Okay." Pratima said and dialed Akash's number. Akash's phone rang.

"Hello maa." Akash said.

"Your papa told me what talks you both had in the morning." Pratima said.

"Hmm." Akash said.

"Akash, we are not pressurising you, son. This is your house and you are most welcome over here. But before giving up, just think twice. It's regarding your career." Pratima said.

"Yes maa."

"Take care." Pratima said and ended the call.

Prashant and Pratima realised that they had done a huge mistake by admitting their son to architecture. They had realised he lacked the idea to make a proper decision. He wasn't a decision-maker.

It was 20th December 2012 when Akash had received a call from Dhaval. His friends were planning a new-year trip to Goa. He wanted to join them as they would be together after a year. But Akash rejected half-heartedly. He couldn't join them because of his college stuff.

The memories of last New Year's party were still fresh in his mind. Akash missed those days a lot. He again wished that if he could rewind the time, just to be with his friends. But he was helpless. Even when his room-mates asked him about the trip, he couldn't reply them.

Akash continued with his college work. Everyday, his friends would give updates regarding their Goa trip such as ticket booking, hotel booking, and much more on the whatsapp group which hurt him the most. He would try to avoid it but somehow he couldn't. Even when they had reached Goa, they would share their pictures and videos everyday which would make Akash almost cry. But he tried his level best to control his emotions and focus on his pending assignments.

Akash's second-semester exams were nearing. But again he had his presentation work and models incomplete for internal markings. He would hear the same complaints as earlier from his professor. After the internal marking, he had tried his level best to cope up with his pending work. But he couldn't make it. Maybe because he was mentally prepared to give up his studies, as he thought.

Akash was getting more upset and worried day by day. He was getting under more pressure, as his exams were nearing. Like everyday, Pratima made a call to him to get his update.

"Nothing is fine maa." Akash said in a low voice. "I don't want to do this."

"Akash, again you have started. Your father has told you that you can come back. But you have to appear for the exams. You are returning after fighting and not just by running away from the problems." Pratima said. Then, Akash took a deep breath and agreed, "Okay."

In the month of April 2012, Akash's last exam had started. Akash would go with his incomplete work and return back. His other classmates, even the ones who had failed along with him, had made better presentation work then him. Then came the last day of his exam. Akash was very heavy hearted as it was his last day at his college while all his other classmates would be continuing the course. After his exam, he went to see his first year's class. The class was empty as the first year's students' exams had ended earlier. He went to the bench on which he used to sit with Shreyas just behind him. He recalled his initial days when he was too excited for a new college life. But sadly he didn't have much happy memories. He wished he could rewind his time. His heart was becoming much heavier. He wanted to cry but he was just stopping his tears from falling off his eyes. He knew he wouldn't be able to control his emotions. So, he left within no time. Even in the evening, he said his final good byes to Amit, Rishabh, Sahil, Ritesh, Rakesh and Kushal before leaving. It was again Amit who had dropped him at the bus stop as Akash had send his scooter to the transporter for sending it to Dhran.

Next day Akash had reached Dhran. Soon, he got ready and reached the dining hall. On seeing him ready, Prashant asked, "Son, take a break for a couple of days and then join." Prashant said.

"Prashant, let him accompany you from today if he wants." Pratima said while passing the plate of paratha towards Akash.

"As you wish." Prashant agreed. Then, soon they had breakfast and went to take Akash's scooter from the transporter. Akash got his scooter and then, he went to the shop along with Prashant.

Prashant and Akash had reached their shop. Akash saw that Prashant's men Chandrakant and Dhiraj lifted the shutters and then started sweeping the floor when Prashant occupied the counter table. He bit Akash to sit next to him. Akash was familiar with the shop. But that day, it felt him completely new as that day he was seeing it from a different perspective – from work point of view.

"For a couple of weeks, you just observe everything. First learn what is called what over here. Then see what the customer demands, how we tackle them, and much more." Prashant said. Then Akash saw three men entering the shop. They were Dilip, Lalit and Saurabh. They also worked over there. "Chandu, Dhiraj, Dilip, Lalit and Saurabh." Prashant called his men. "From now onwards, Akash is with us. First, just show him all the basic things and guide him to handle the customers." Then he turned towards Akash and said, "Even you try to be with them as much as possible. Be with them when they go to the go-down or when they are handling the customers."

"Okay papa." Akash said. Then he saw some customers entering the shop.

Akash was hesitant to inform his friends that he was back to Dhran. He didn't know where to start. But somehow, he send a message in his friends' whatsapp group during his lunch time, stating that he had left his studies and joined his father on his business. After reading his message, everyone was left startled. They started asking him the reason. But Akash could just type that he was at his shop at that time and would explain everything in the evening.

The whole day went on. Akash would just observe what the customers wanted and how his father and his men provided them the required goods. He saw that mostly the painters and very rarely the house owners visited them. He even saw that some of the painters were asking for some kind of charges from his father, and his father paid them the amount. He didn't know for what that was. At the day's end, he had learned most of the products' name.

Prashant and Akash had returned home in the evening. While they had sat for the dinner, Pratima brought the novels which Janhvi and Tejas had given to Akash. She placed the novels on the table near him. Akash couldn't believe his eyes. "I thought you have returned this books to Janhvi aunty."

"I was going to return. But she refused. She told me to let it be with you." Pratima said while having her chair. "Now read it and understand it completely."

"Thank you very much maa." Akash said. He was very much thankful for such a supportive and understanding parents. He was very happy on receiving the novels back. So, after the dinner, he straight away took the novels to his bedroom and started reading the fourth book of the series which Tejas had given to him. None of Akash's childhood friends were in Dhran. Some were doing for post-graduation while some were busy with their jobs. So, he had ample of time to spend behind the book.

"How was Akash's first day?" Pratima asked Prashant while readying the bed.

"He will need some time. Don't worry Pratima. He will get on track." Prashant said.

Akash again had a new beginning. He knew that he had to handle his father's shop and side-by-side focus on his writing. So, he had made a schedule which began from the day's start till its end. He would get up at six o'clock in the morning, get ready, pray, have breakfast by himself, and by quarter to seven he would sit with his reading work till half past eight. By quarter to nine, he would reach his shop when his men would be lifting the shutters and sweeping the floor. By nine o'clock, the shop would start.

Akash would spend his whole day in his father's shop, trying to learn the ways of doing business. Then, by eight o'clock in the evening, he and Prashant would reach home. Akash would get fresh, have his dinner, and by half past eight, he would continue his reading work. Then by ten o'clock, he would go to bed. He could have continued reading till late at night, but he believed that he needed proper sleep to focus on his writing work.

Akash tried to stick himself firmly on his schedule, because he didn't want to give up on writing just like architecture. But that just made him be only at his home and shop. He would not go anywhere else as he lacked time. He wanted to finish his reading work and start writing his own novel as soon as possible. Even after some days, he got to know that two historic television serials had started, out of which one was on the life of Mewad king Maharana Pratap and the other was on the life of Maurya emperor Ashoka. He would watch those serials without fail as he loved history very much.

Once, while Akash was with his books, Prashant silently walked into his room just to pay him a visit.

"Oh, papa! I didn't see you." Akash said as he was surprised to see Prashant in his room.

"The whole day you are either at the shop or in your room with your books. What are you upto, son?" Prashant asked.

"I was just reading this novel." Akash said.

"Akash, I know you love reading and you are planning to write a book. But for a while, take out time for yourself, son. Go out and make friends. The more you will get contacts, the more you will get to learn what is going on in this world." Prashant was explaining to him. "Your contacts will help you a lot in attaining success. You want to write a book. Who will read your book if no one knows you out there? Just think about it."

"Okay papa." Akash said blindly.

"Even on Sundays, you are just with your books the whole day. Things don't work like this, boy." Prashant said. He gave a radiant smile, hoping that Akash would have understood. Then he left the room.

CHAPTER SEVEN

Akash continued with his reading work. He didn't know whether he understood Prashant's words or not. He didn't understand why he needed huge contacts to be a successful writer. He was under the impression that he just needed a good story and a good publisher to make his book happen.

While Akash was busy with his reading work, his phone rang. He saw that his friends had made a whatsapp group call and he knew for what. He received the call and saw everyone on his mobile phone's screen. "Hey everyone." He said while closing his bedroom's door. He was shy for sharing his communication with his parents.

They were discussing about Akash's giving up his studies. Akash explained them everything that it was not the field of Akash's choice. He was learning his father's business and side-by-side planning to write a novel

"What novel?" Ankita asked. Everyone had the same question.

"Actually it's a fiction-fantasy novel." Akash said. "Actually right now, I am reading books of the similar genre. I am getting the glimpse of how it is to be written. Then I will start writing."

"That sounds great." Manish said.

"We will be waiting for your book." Rohan said to which everyone eagerly agreed. Everyone seemed excited for his book. Then, they had a good talk for a while before ending the call. By then, it was ten o'clock. So, Akash put his book mark in his novel, closed it and went to sleep.

After almost six months, Akash had completed reading all the novels and noting down the difficult words with their meanings. He had completely understood both the stories. Then, he had started writing his own novel. First, he wrote down the outline of the story, from where the story started, from where it passed and where it ended.

The days went on. Akash would work on his novel in the morning and evening every day and spend his day at his shop. But there seemed one trouble. Akash was getting addicted to something, something more harmful than drugs or alcohol. It was social media. Akash was getting addicted towards social media. Whenever Akash would get time while being in his shop, he would take out his mobile phone from his pocket and start surfing it.

"Akash, stop using your mobile and concentrate on your work." Prashant would always yell at him whenever he would use his mobile during work hours. Even at home, while he would sit with his writing work, he would spend half of his time on social media. By this he would miss every deadline for every chapter he would decide.

Then, again it was mid-December. When Akash was at his shop, he had received a call from Ankita. Akash's friends were planning a new-year trip to Daman. So, Ankita was asking his confirmation as he missed the group discussion on their whatsapp group. To that, Akash eagerly agreed.

"What are you all planning?" Prashant asked.

"Papa, we are planning to go to Daman on this new-year's eve. We will leave on 31st by car and return on 6th. So, can I go?" Akash asked.

"Yeah, sure." Prashant said happily. He knew that his son really needed to go out of the walls of his house, to know and understand the world. And that was the perfect time.

It was 30th of December. Everyone had reached Dhran. It was still early morning, so everyone wanted to meet. They all gathered but Akash wasn't there. "Where is Akash?" Dhaval asked.

"He is working on his book." Tejas said. "I convinced him to come down, but he wants to do his writing work."

"Let's go inside and drag him out." Manish japed. So, he and Dhaval went inside Akash's house to call him.

"Hey Mr. Writer, we know you are very serious about your novel. Now take some break and come with us." Manish said as they entered Akash's room. Akash was writing his book at that time.

"Guys, you all carry on. I really need to complete this book." Akash said halfheartedly. He wanted to join them, but he couldn't.

"You aren't going to complete your book by today, are you?" Dhaval asked. "Buddy, we don't meet everyday like this."

"Guys, I really want to join you, but I am missing all the deadlines. And as it is from tomorrow we are there together."

"Dude come on. We too have left our work for this trip." Manish tried to persuade him.

"Guys, please try to understand." Akash said while trying to explain him his so-called situation. Manish and Dhaval stared at him in amazement as it seemed weird to them. So, they just said 'Okay' to him and left. Then, Akash saw Prashant entering his room. Prashant was outside his room, hearing their conversation.

"Son, I have told you earlier and again I will be repeating. Your career in important, but making friends and being socialize is much more important. Even though you make a good career, you are nothing without your friend circle." Prashant tried to explain him. "Just imagine, you have completed your book and there is no one to buy it. Your friends are the first one to buy it and you are avoiding them. Try to understand this, son." Prashant placed his hand on Akash's head to support him. Then he left the room.

Next day, Akash's alarm rang at three o'clock in the morning. He rubbed his sleep from his eyes and put off the alarm. While still being in his half sleep, he got ready within fifteen minutes and started waking up Tejas. "Tejas, wake up, it's almost time."

"Hmmm..... Bhaiya......... no one is going to be on time." Tejas said in his half sleep. He wasn't getting up. So, he went down to have his breakfast. Pratima was already up to make their breakfast.

"Are you sure you all will be leaving so early?" Pratima asked.

"Yes maa. We have decided before hand." Akash said. After his breakfast, he was waiting for everyone to come out. Only five minutes were remaining to leave but none was out. He went up to wake up Tejas, but he had already went to the washroom. Then he send a message to his friends on their whatsapp group, stating to get ready. But none replied. That made him realise that no one was up. So he started calling everyone one-by-one. First he called Dhaval.

"Hmm." Dhaval replied while still in his half sleep.

"Have you woken up or not?" Akash asked.

"Hmm..... Who's this?" Dhaval asked. He had still not opened his eyes.

"You idiot. It's me, Akash." Akash snapped.

"Oh! Yeah. I am.... Almost ready." Dhaval said while rubbing his eyes.

"You are waking up right now!" Akash was shocked.

"Yeah, just give me fifteen minutes." Dhaval said and ended the call. Then Akash called everyone one-by-one and got to know that everyone was waking up after he called them. Then after an hour, everyone was out with their luggage. Akash realised that he was a fool, who was woken up like an owl while everyone else was sleeping.

It was too cold outside. So, they were wearing jackets and all sort of woolen wears.

"Guys, we were supposed to leave by four." Akash said as he reached outside.

"You must have finished your book, mustn't you?" Ankita teased Akash.

"Guys, our Akash is so hardworking that even after writing his novel the whole day, he was ready by four o'clock." Dhruv japed. Akash just looked on without any reply. Then, to change the topic, he said, "Guys, we are already one hour late."

"Yeah, Akash doesn't like to miss deadlines. So guys, hurry up." Rohan giggled and so, everyone had a laugh while Akash looked on.

"Akash, we are on a vacation and not for your novel's audition. So, just chill." Manisha said. "But where are Dhaval and Manish?"

"They are getting their cars out." Tejas said. Soon, Dhaval and Manish had brought their seven seated SUV cars out. They got divided into two group and got arranged in both the cars. And their journey began.

Everyone was very excited for Daman as well as the road trip. They did all sort of fun and took pictures. It was six hours journey. Everyone was feeling sleepy, especially Akash. But they were too busy doing fun. Even the highway was having six lanes. So, they enjoyed the drive very much. Then after sometime, they had reached Navapur, a town on Maharashtra – Gujarat border. They wanted to have patra bhajiyas over there. So, they stopped at one of the restaurants, got fresh and had a lot of patra bhajiyas.

Again, they started their journey towards Daman. They had even packed some of the patra bhajiyas for having it in their journey. Then by noon, they had reached Daman. While they were on their way towards their hotel, they saw that the town was very beautiful, having Portuguese style architecture at several places. Then, they had reached their hotel.

After reaching the hotel, Akash and his friends had got their room. But, as soon as they entered, they were left startled. The room was too big with ten single beds in it. They had done online registration for such a kind of room, but still they were amazed.

"Wow." Everyone said as they entered the room.

"This is really amazing." Akash said. Then, each one of them had their beds. Then, within sometime, everyone got ready, had their lunch in the restaurant and then went to the beach.

The beach was at the backside of the hotel. "Akash, why are you wearing jeans on beach?" Ankita asked as she saw Akash in jeans.

"Why are you asking this?" Akash asked as he was bemused.

"Haven't you brought shorts?" Minakshi asked. Akash saw that everyone was wearing shorts except him.

"Oh!" He said.

"We are on a vacation, Akash. We should have vacation's mood." Sejal said but Akash couldn't reply. He wondered why was he like that, taking time to understand things and the situation. He was hurt a bit, but he let it go. Then, they had reached the beach.

The beach was very beautiful with almost no crowd on it. The main beach of Daman was far away. They had planned to visit it the next day.

Akash and his friends were enjoying on the beach a lot. Akash was seeing the beach for the first time and that turned out to be his best experience. They took pictures over there and had all sort of fun.

Then, it was evening. While Akash and his friends were moving towards their room, they saw people moving towards the party ground.

"Has the party begun?" Tejas asked.

"May be." Dhruv said. So, they furtively went towards their room, got ready and immediately went to the party. Even before reaching the party, they didn't forget to take photographs. Then, they reached the ground.

The party ground was too huge. Akash and his friends were astonished to see the huge stage, the disco lights and all sort of arrangements. They hadn't seen such a luxurious party before.

The party had already begun with people dancing widely on the music and having drinks all around. Akash and his friends felt a bit awkward for being around drinkers. But still they joined the dance.

The music was going on loud and wild. People were screaming out of their lungs while dancing passionately. Everyone was enjoying a lot.

Then, it was mid-night. The music suddenly stopped and so the dance and shouting. The DJ announced loudly about the new-year's arrival with fire crackers bursting all over the sky. The folks started shouting – *HAPPY NEW YEAR*. Akash and his friends too did the same. Then, again the music started and so, the dance and the shouts.

Akash had started enjoying his life. He had realised life is all about enjoying the present and not about complaining about the past. He would forget all of his problems whenever he would be with his childhood friends.

CHAPTER EIGHT

The party was over. Next morning, everyone had decided to leave by eight o'clock, but none was up by that time as everyone was tired. As usual, Akash was the first one to get up. He was ready by nine. Then he had started waking up everyone. "Guys, it's already nine o'clock. Wake up." But none of them replied. Again he realised that he was such a fool. Then, after some time, everyone started waking up and by eleven o'clock they were ready.

Everyone had brunch and left for the sightseeing. They spent the whole day visiting the beaches, forts and all the tourist spots in the city. The rest of the days they spent the same. Then, on 6th of January, they returned back to Dhran.

Akash was back to his routine after reaching Dhran. In the morning, he would sit with his writing work, then spend his day at his shop and again sit with his writing work in the evening. He would even spend his Sundays on his writing work. He had made his life boring with absolutely no entertainment. He would get frustrated by his schedule sometimes, but he hadn't made any other option for himself. The only relief for him was Dhaval, who had returned from Pune and joined his father's business.

The days went on. But the next chapter of Akash's life was about to start. His parents had selected a girl for him. Her name was Neha, who stayed in Dhran with her family.

The day had arrived when both the families had planned to meet at Neha's place. It was in the evening when Akash and his parents had reached there. As they reached there, they were given a warm welcome by Neha's father – Amish and her four brothers – Abhimanyu, Yash, Meghraj and Abhishek. But as they entered, they were astonished to see a three storied luxurious bungalow with a beautiful garden where several cars and numerous bikes, scooters and bicycles were parked at the ground floor. They had realised Neha's family's status.

"Welcome Prashantji and Pratimaji." Amish said while joining hands with a broad smile.

"Thank you Amishji." Prashant said while they too joined their hands happily. Then, they were let inside the house.

Akash was really impressed by the beautiful interior of the house. Everyone had their seats in the living room and started their talks. But Akash was a bit nervous. He had a nice talk with Amish. But he didn't know how he would start conversation with Neha. Then, Akash saw a girl coming downstairs along with her mother and her younger sister. He had realised that she was Neha. Akash got a bit tensed. They had their seats next to Amish.

"She is my daughter – Neha." Amish said while pointing towards the girl. Then he added while pointing towards his wife and younger daughter, "She is my wife – Tamanna and she is my younger daughter – Fulki." Akash looked at Neha, but she turned her eyes down in blush. Then, they both were asked whether they wanted to talk or not. So, they both agreed and went inside Neha's bedroom to share some words.

As Akash entered Neha's room along with her, he saw that it was very systematic and tidy. He even saw that badminton rackets and lawn tennis rackets were arranged in one corner, some novels were kept on the shelves and some files were arranged on her table.

"Hello." Akash said nervously.

"Hi." Neha replied.

"Ah..... You can ask me anything." Akash said while trying to be confident.

"What do you expect from a wife?" Neha asked confidently as she knew she had all the qualities of a perfect wife. Akash had not expected such type of questions. Still he replied, "Just a good nature. That's it."

"Okay." Neha replied. She was expecting a long list but was shocked to hear such a small reply. She had realised Akash was a bit hesitant.

"What do you expect from a husband?" Akash asked.

"He should be caring, supportive, loyal, down to earth, and a responsible person. He should be the one in whom people see a leader. I am not expecting a good looking or a rich husband, but a husband who has the guts to move forward in life." Neha said. But Akash was shocked to hear those words. He knew he was just down to earth and loyal, but wasn't sure about the other qualities. His confidence was a bit shaken and Neha could see it on his face. "Shall I get you a glass of water?" She asked to comfort him.

"No thanks." Akash said.

"So, what are your qualification?" Neha asked. But this time, Akash felt that he was in some exam hall. He didn't have a degree and he felt that, that would spoil his image in front of her. But still he said, "I was doing architecture, but I couldn't complete it. But now I have joined my father's business."

"That's great." Neha said encouragingly, trying to make Akash more confident. "But why are you so nervous?"

"No, I am comfortable." Akash tried to control his nervousness. "What are your qualifications?"

"I have done M.B.A., and now I am working as an accountant at Kharwanda Hospital." Neha said confidently.

"Oh, that's great." Akash said. He was again startled. Neha had received her master's degree and was doing a job at a reputed hospital while he didn't have even a bachelor's degree. Akash was a bit embarrassed.

"What are your hobbies?" Neha asked.

"Reading and writing." Akash replied. "Actually I am writing a fiction – fantasy novel."

"Oh! That's great. Let me know when you complete it." Neha said excitedly.

"Yeah, sure." Akash said eagerly. "By the way, what are your hobbies?"

"I like reading, swimming, cycling, playing lawn tennis, cricket, basketball and badminton, yoga, tracking, cooking, photography, and..........." Neha gave a guess. "There is a lot of stuff. Actually my daily routine is – I get up at five o'clock in the morning, do yoga for an hour, then go for lawn tennis, and then swimming. The tennis court and swimming pool are nearby. Then by eight o'clock, I am back to home. I have my breakfast and get ready. By nine o'clock, I reach my work place and by around six o'clock I am again at home. Then for a couple of hour, I go for cycling with my friends throughout the town. By eight o'clock, we have our dinner. Then, till nine o'clock it's our family time. Then, from nine – ten, I read novels, and then go to bed."

"Oh, that's........really amazing." Akash was impressed.

"Do you still have anything more to ask?" Neha asked.

"Don't you want to ask anything regarding my degree?" Akash asked nervously.

"No, you have cleared everything." Neha gave a radiant smile. But Akash was still bemused. So, Neha added, "Akash, what I feel is, degree is important, but what counts is your passion to move forward in life even if you don't have a degree. So, don't worry. I will not judge you on the basis of your education. But I might judge you on the basis of your career planning."

"Okay." Akash said. "Shall we move out?"

"Yeah sure." Neha said. So, they moved out of their room. As they came out, Akash saw that Neha's four sister-in-laws were also seated next to their husbands. They were Raashi, Mamta, Niharika and Aarna. They had brought some snacks for everyone.

"Come both of you. Have your seats." Amish said to Akash and Neha.

"By the way Akash, what are you doing right now?" Amish said.

"Actually we are having oil paints' business." Prashant said while having his samosa. Neha was expecting Akash to reply, but he was just busy in having bhajiyas and tea which she felt a bit a droll.

"Oh that's great. Even my eldest son Abhimanyu is handling our oil paints' business." Amish said. "Actually we are having four businesses and all my four sons are handling them. Abhimanyu is looking after oil paints' business, Yash is looking after hardware's business, Meghraj is looking after plywood's business, and Abhishek is looking after glass' business. Neha is doing accountant's job in Kharwanda hospital while Fulki is doing her graduation."

"Oh, that's really great." Prashant said as he was impressed by their business setup. Then after sometime, both the families greeted each-other and ended the meeting. Then, Akash and his parents left.

"Did you like the girl?" Pratima asked Akash while they were on their way.

"Yes maa." Akash said. So, Prashant and Pratima realised that Akash was ready for the marriage. Even on the next day, Neha's parents had called Prashant and Pratima to give their confirmation about their marriage.

Akash and Neha had exchanged their mobile number. On the first day, Akash was very nervous to call her. So, after the dinner, he straight away went to his room to call her.

Akash was too hesitant to talk to Neha. Their talks started with 'hello, how are you, how is everyone at home.' Neha had realised that he didn't have words to talk and so, she felt a bit droll about it. "How was your day?" She asked.

"Fine." Akash replied in one word. Neha was wondering that how come Akash's day was just 'Fine'. If he would have asked, then she would have told a long story about her day from morning till the evening. She had expected the same from him. But he just said 'Fine' an ended the sentence.

"Okay then." Neha said.

"Bye." Akash said and ended the call.

While lying on the bed, Neha was just wondering about Akash's call. He had end the call too early. Why was he so nervous and shy, she wondered. Would she be able to spend her whole life with him if he stayed like that, she didn't know.

After somedays, their parents had decided a day for their engagement. They were engaged with all the rituals done right. That day too, Akash was strung for the new beginning. Neha had noticed his anxiousness on his face but didn't utter a word.

"Are you comfortable?" Neha asked Akash secretly during the photo-shoot.

"Yeah, I am all right." Akash replied while trying to be confident. But Neha had realised that she was marrying a wrong person.

The days went on. Akash would spend his morning on his book, his day at his shop and evening again on his book. Then, he would go to his room after the dinner and talk to Neha just for ten – fifteen minutes. Once while talking, Neha impatiently asked, "Why do you talk so less?"

"I don't know." Akash said hesitantly.

"But it's only me who is talking. You hardly talk." Neha said impatiently. But Akash could just hold his head without a word. "Okay, let it be. I am ending the call." Neha ended the call out of frustration.

Akash was getting too much depressed regarding his relationship. He didn't know what he was lacking. He would just wish for a time rewind, so that he would start writing his novel at the age of sixteen, finish it as soon as possible and be a successful writer before his marriage. But now, he was stuck between his business, novel writing, friends and relationship. He wasn't good at any of those. He lacked communication skills.

It was 15th March. Akash didn't call Neha that day as he wanted to give her a surprise call on mid-night for her birthday. Neha was waiting for Akash's call in the evening. She thought that he must have forgotten. How he could forget to call her, she thought. Then, she gave up the idea for waiting for his call.

It was mid-night. The doorbell rang. Neha knew her friends must have visited to wish her. She was right. As she opened the door, everyone shouted, "HAPPY BIRTHDAY." Neha's friends Amisha, Rasika, Jahnvi, and Fulmala had visited.

"Thank you." Neha said while hugging her friends. "Come inside." She added and let everyone enter. Even Fulki had joined them.

"Where are bhaiyas and bhabis?" Rasika asked while placing the cake on the table.

"They are off to bed." Neha said.

"But where is jiju?" Fulmala asked.

"He hasn't come." Neha said. She was expecting Akash to give her a surprise, but she wasn't sure whether he knew her birthday or not. She wasn't supposed to feel depressed in front of her friends. But suddenly her phone rang, and to her surprise, she saw that it was Akash's call.

"Hello." Neha said excitedly.

"A very happy birthday to you." Akash said.

"Thank you." Neha said happily. "Did you know it?"

"Yes of course. How could I forget this day?" Akash said. "So, what's the plan for today?" Neha was startled to hear that. She was expecting Akash to plan something for her. But instead of that, he was asking her about her plans.

"Nothing such." Neha replied.

"Okay, enjoy your day." Akash said. Again, Neha was expecting Akash to continue their talks, but he was ending the call.

"Okay, bye." Neha said and ended the call. Fulki saw Neha's happy face turning sad. But she didn't utter a word in front of her friends.

"Neha, will you cut the cake or shall we do it for you?" Rasika Japed. So, Neha cut the cake and celebrated her birthday.

After her friends were gone, Neha straight away went to her room. As she laid on her bed, Fulki asked, "Didi, why were you so upset after talking to jiju?"

"Fulki, just go to sleep." Neha said with her closed eyes.

"You can share it with me." Fulki persuaded.

"It was all my fault. I was expecting too much from Akash." Neha said in disguise. "I thought that he would come here and give me a surprise with a cake and a gift. But he just made a formal call. Then he was asking me that what my plans are for today." She paused for a second and continued, "I mean, he can't even plan something on my birthday. He doesn't have any plans for anything, be it any occasion or his own career. Huh!" Neha was trying to stop her tears in her eyes. Even Fulki had no words. So, they both just switched off the lights and went to sleep.

Next day was same as usual for Akash. But Neha was flooded with wishes followed by cake cutting at her hospital. She had a great day.

In the evening, Neha had planned to go on a dinner with her friends. The doorbell rang. She thought that those must be her friends. But to her surprise, it was Akash.

"Oh, hi! What a pleasant surprise!" Neha said as she wasn't expecting Akash.

"Happy birthday." Akash wished her. Neha's full family came to meet him.

"HEY!" Everyone heard some girls calling from the entrance. Everyone saw that Neha's friends had come.

"Actually Akash, we have planned to go for a dinner. So, why don't you join us?" Neha asked.

"Oh!" Akash was a bit shocked. He had planned a date with Neha, but was unaware of her plan. Still, he agreed to join them.

"I hadn't expected that you would give me a surprise visit." Neha said while they rode towards the restaurant.

"Oh!" Akash said. He gave a reactionless look. Then, Akash went on riding the scooter the whole way without a word with Neha. It was only Neha who was going on talking and Akash would give just one word reply. Neha was expecting him to talk more, but he didn't. Then, they reached the restaurant.

Even while selecting the menu at the restaurant, it was Neha who asked Akash what he would like to have. "Sev-bhaji, Kaju-curry and Chapatti." Akash replied. So, Neha just gave a blank look at him. "What?" Akash asked while giving a baffled look.

"Nothing." Neha said in disguise. She was expecting him to ask her what she wanted. Even her friends exchanged bemused looks with her.

Soon, the dinner was over. The waiter brought the bill and placed it near Akash. "Shall we divide the bill?" Akash asked blankly as he saw the bill. But Neha was startled to hear that. She thought that Akash, being her fiancé, would pay the bill.

"Yeah sure." Jahnvi said and so, they divided the amount and paid the bill. Then, they had left the restaurant and were about to move towards their home when Neha said, "Guys, you all leave. I and Akash are going for a ride."

"Oho." Everyone teased her.

"Neha, aren't we getting late?" Akash asked dumbly. So, again Neha glared at him in astonishment.

"Enjoy your ride and take care." Fulmala said.

"Yeah, bye." Neha said while her friends left.

"Let us move." Neha said to Akash and so, they too left.

"Where are we supposed to go?" Akash asked while riding.

"Am I supposed to tell you where are we supposed to go?" Neha asked out of frustration. "What's wrong with you Akash?"

"What's wrong with me?" Akash asked as he was bemused.

"It's only me who is always talking. Why don't you talk?" Neha asked. Her anger was bursting out of her.

"I do talk." Akash confirmed.

"Oh really! You just end your talk in one line or one word." Neha said. "You don't know how to talk, you don't know how to be with your fiancée, you don't even ask what I want to eat, you don't want to go on a long ride. Is this how you celebrate your fiancée's birthday?"

Akash was wordless. He didn't know where he was going wrong. Soon, they had reached where roadside sitting arrangements were done. Neha bid Akash to stop so that they would sit over there and share their words.

"Today is my birthday Akash. Being my fiancé, you were supposed to pay the bill." Neha said with disappointment. "But instead, you are asking my friends to contribute."

Akash realised his mistakes. But before he could say anything, Neha interjected, "I had asked you what you would like to have. Wasn't it your responsibility to ask me what I wanted? Everyone was expecting that from you?"

Akash didn't have any words. He was just blankly staring at Neha. "Relations doesn't work like this Akash. In the first meeting I had cleared what I expect from a husband."

"I am sorry Neha. This won't happen next time." Akash said while holding her hands. But Neha pulled back her hands. She was too much frustrated. She wanted to say that it was useless talking to him. But still she took a deep breath said, "I am giving you last chance."

"I understand." Akash said.

"Now let's move." Neha said and stood up. Then they moved towards their home.

Akash had realised his mistake. While lying on his bed, he was wondering why he was no dumb. He wished that if he could get just one chance to rewind the time and be where he was when he was sixteen, so that he would build a proper career and correct all the mistakes which he had done. But none could rewind the time. So, he just went to sleep.

CHAPTER NINE

'Tik – Tik.' The morning five o'clock alarm rang. Neha woke up from her sleep and put off the alarm. Then she furtively went to brush her teeth as she didn't want to miss any minute for her yoga session. Within five minutes, she was out. She immediately took her yoga mat and went to the terrace for yoga. At that time, Akash was in his deep sleep.

Then, the six o'clock alarm rang. Akash woke up to get ready, while Neha packed her yoga mat, placed it back in her cupboard, took her lawn-tennis racket and moved out. The sports' complex was opposite to her house. So, within a couple of minutes, she was there. Even all her friends joined her. They played over there for an hour.

By seven o'clock, Akash was with his book, while Neha and her friends had moved for swimming. The swimming pool was there in the same complex.

By eight o'clock, Neha had reached home. First, she went to take bath, got ready and had her breakfast. Then, at half past eight, Akash had left for his shop. Even Neha had left for her hospital by quarter to nine.

By nine o'clock, both of them were on their work tables. Akash was still struggling to handle the business. He was just physically present, but his mind was fixed on the books. Even he was too addicted to social media and so, that day Prashant warned him to stay away from his mobile phone. Even Neha was trying her level best to manage all the account throughout the day.

By six o'clock in the evening, Neha had left for her home. As soon as she reached home, she got fresh and went for cycling along with her friends who were already waiting for her at the gate. They roamed the whole town and had a good chat while riding, discussing their whole day. Neha was very fond of cycling, yoga, sports, and reading. She believed that she gained happiness and positivity only by keeping her body and mind healthy.

By eight o'clock, both Akash and Neha had reached home. They both got fresh and finished their dinner by half-past-eight. Then, Akash went to his bedroom and started writing his novels, while Neha's family gathered in the living room to watch their favourite television show. Neha's family enjoyed a lot while spending the time together.

By nine o'clock, Neha went to her room and started reading her novels. And then, by ten o'clock, Akash called Neha as usual. They had a talk for ten minutes and then, both went to sleep. Akash and Neha used to follow that routine everyday.

It was May. During his working hours, Akash saw a message of Dhruv in their friends group stating everyone to be present in Dhran on the coming weekend along with their fiancés and fiancées. Everyone in the group was excited as well as bemused. They all asked him about the matter. Even Akash asked made a call to him to ask him what had happened.

"It's a surprise for everyone." Dhaval said. So, Akash didn't give much though and ended the call. He was excitedly waiting for the weekend as everyone would be together after a long time.

Then, Friday arrived. Even Tejas had reached home. Everyone had reached Dhran in the morning. So, they got ready and went out in the colony to meet each other after a long time. Ankita's fiancé Harshal, Nitya's fiancé Pradeep, Minakshi's fiancé Dinesh, Prajakta, and Manisha had also arrived. Everyone was meeting Harshal, Pradeep and Dinesh for the first time. Over there, they again asked Dhaval the reason behind their get-together.

"Tonight, I am giving you a party at Hotel Olive. Over there, I will reveal everything." Dhaval said.

In the evening, everyone had gathered in the colony to go for the dinner. Akash had brought Neha over there. Neha was meeting Akash's friends for the first time and she was very much pleased. Again before leaving, everyone asked Dhruv the reason for the party.

"Guys, have patience. You will learn soon." Dhruv said.

"He is definitely getting engaged." Minakshi Japed.

"No ways. I am not going to celebrate for that." Dhruv said. So, everyone had a guffaw. Then, they moved towards the hotel. As they reached the hotel and booked the table over there, Dhruv made an announcement.

"Guys, there is a good news which I need to tell you." Dhruv announced. Everyone was eagerly listening to him. "I have started my new software firm under the name – Digilutions, in Bengaluru."

"Oho! Congratulations." Everyone congratulated Dhruv for his new venture. They were happy for Dhruv as he was the first one amongst them to start a new firm.

While on their way back home, Neha asked Akash, "Why don't you start a side business of your own?" But Akash just gave a pause, wondering what she meant. "Look at Dhruv. How happy and confident he is, just because he has started a new firm on his own."

"But I too am writing a novel." Akash said.

"Yeah, but writing is not everything. Do you know anything regarding publishing and marketing?" Neha asked. "For your book, you have to create audience. And for creating audience, you have to create contacts."

Akash wondered why Neha was telling him all that. He was still under the impression that his work was just writing, and the rest was publisher's work.

As the days passed, Akash realised that he didn't have just one but many flaws regarding his presence of mind, personality, caring, etc. The more his flaws came out, the more he would have arguments with Neha.

One such moment was, their marriage dates were fixed. It was in mid-November, when their parents had decided their dates with all the rituals. The dates were in first week of January 2015. Both Akash and Neha were heralded by their parents. Akash just took it in a normal way but Neha was tensed a lot. She didn't know how she would manage with Akash after the marriage. She was waiting the whole day, expecting Akash to give her the news. But that didn't happen until it was evening when Akash called as always.

As usual, Akash began with 'hello' and 'how are you'. So, Neha got frustrated, "Aren't you going to start a new topic or just keep on asking the same question everyday?"

"Neha, what's wrong?" Akash asked out of dismay.

"What's wrong! Huh! By the way, our marriage dates are fixed and I know you won't bother to inform me." Neha said. Her temper was on the rise.

"Oh please Neha, I was going to tell you." Akash said. This time, he was resting his forehead on his palm.

"Oh really! When? After our wedding?" Neha taunted. But Akash was at a loss for words. "I am ending the call. Bye."

"Ne....." Akash was about to stop her. But she ended the call.

Akash couldn't figure out why he was like that. Everyday, everything would happen in the perfect way. But in the end, his irresponsible behavior would spoil everything. He was proving himself the same everywhere – be it in relationships, business, or at home. Neha was on the verge of breaking the relationship, but it was due to Akash who took her on a dinner date and gifted her a mobile phone as an apology.

Then, it was Akash's birthday on the 5th of December. At midnight, Neha had called him just like his friends to wish him. Akash had remembered what blunder he had done on Neha's birthday. So, he had planned everything that day effectively. In the afternoon, he had made a call to Neha and asked her about dinner.

"Of course, it's your special day today." Neha agreed.

Then, in the evening, Akash got ready in the best way possible and went to pick up Neha. But, as he reached at Neha's place, he saw that Neha had already arranged a cake-cutting program over there.

"HAPPY BIRTHDAY." The whole family wished.

"Thank you so much everyone." Akash replied happily.

"Come inside." Neha said. So, Akash moved further inside the living room and saw that it was beautifully decorated with a 'Happy Birthday' banner on the wall and a cake on the table.

"Oh! Thank you so much Neha." Akash said as he was amazed to see the preparation. He had his seat and asked Neha to sit beside him. Then, he cut the cake.

"Happy birthday to you." Everyone started singing and then, Akash and Neha fed the cake bites to each other. They even took pictures with everyone.

"Akash! This is for you." Amish said as he and Tamanna got him a gift.

"Oh! Thank you." Akash said while unboxing the gift. It was a dark blue jeans and a formal apple-cut checked shirt and a wrist watch. "Oh! This is really nice." Then, Akash and Neha left.

"Where are we going?" Neha asked while they were on the way.

"One of my school-mates has started a restaurant by 'Taste buds' name near Jai Bharat College. We are going over there." Akash said.

Soon, they had reached the restaurant. It was a beautiful restaurant made out of two huge metal containers placed on the either side of a wooden deck. The wooden deck was having an open air seating, while one of the containers had A/C seating and the other one was the kitchen.

Harshwardhan, the owner of the restaurant and Akash's school-mate, came to wish Akash for his birthday.

"Thank you very much." Akash said while hugging him. He even introduced Neha to him. Then, he led them inside towards their reserved table on the deck.

"What would you like to have?" Akash asked Neha as he opened the menu card and turned towards her.

"Sev-bhaji, Kaju-curry and chapatti." Neha japed. Akash realised that Neha was teasing him. So, they both had a guffaw.

Akash and Neha had a great time over there. After the dinner, they went for a long ride and had some dessert.

It was already mid-night when Akash dropped Neha home. Akash had started liking her, but Neha was still confused. Then, Akash exchanged a mutual smile with her, said good-bye and left.

Their wedding day was nearing. They had done all kind of shopping regarding their clothes, shoes, and all the required items. Their parents had also started distributing the cards.

Once on the call, Neha asked Akash about their honeymoon plan. But Akash just replied, "I haven't decided yet."

"What!" Neha was startled. "Akash, only few days are left for our marriage and still you haven't decided anything regarding our honeymoon."

"What's the issue in that?" Akash asked.

"What's the issue!" Neha exclaimed. "Akash, it's our honeymoon." Neha was the person who was dreaming of travelling the whole world just like her brothers and sister-in-laws. But Akash wasn't prepared for any trip.

"Okay, I will talk to papa and let you know by tomorrow." Akash said.

"Anyways, what about our pre-wedding photo-shoot?" Neha asked.

"What's that?" Akash got bemused. So, Neha held her forehead in disguise and said, "Akash, why are you marrying me and destroying my life?"

"Now what is wrong with you?" Akash asked.

"I am marrying you. That's wrong with me." Neha said out of frustration and ended the call.

Akash and Neha were getting more depressed. Their wedding day was nearing and they were totally blank about how they would deal with each other.

Next day, Akash was busy searching the honeymoon destinations online. Then, he finalized going to Kerala. He had visited one of the tour operators' site and downloaded the itinerary. Then in the evening, he called Neha and asked for her P.A.N. card and Adharcard, as he wanted to do the registration.

"But, don't you need the passport?" Neha asked.

"No, just the Adharcard and P.A.N. card." Akash said.

"Where are we going?" Neha asked.

"We are going to Kerala." Amit said excitedly.

"Oh!" Neha said. She was unhappy. She was expecting Akash to ask her about where she wanted to go. But still, she had accepted the trip unwillingly.

The days went on. Finally Akash and Neha were married on 11th January 2015. But there was a twist on their wedding night. They had a good talk when they were in their room. But, as Akash tried to near her, she stopped him. Akash stared at her in amazement. He wondered about what was wrong again.

"Akash, I don't think so our relation is that strong as required. Please don't mind my words, but we still need some time." Neha said. Akash paused for a couple of seconds and then agreed. They both exchanged formal smiles, switched off the lights and went to sleep.

While lying on the bed, Akash wondered about what was missing between them to be a good couple. He turned towards Neha who was fast asleep facing in the opposite direction. He wanted to cuddle her and tell her how much he loved her. They were the couple just for the world. They didn't know how much time they needed to understand each other.

CHAPTER TEN

Next morning was a bit different for Akash and Neha. It was their first morning together. All the guest in the house were ready to leave. Even they both were had left for Mumbai in the evening, as they had flight to Kochi the next day.

Akash was too excited for the honeymoon trip, but Neha wasn't. On the way towards Mumbai, she had an argument over the location. But she had to swallow her temper as they were travelling with other passengers in the bus.

In Mumbai, Akash and Neha had reached the airport on time. They both were travelling in the plane for the first time. Neha was adventurous. So, she was too excited to sit in the plane. She had purposely bit Akash to book a window seat for her. But Akash was a bit nervous. He didn't like heights. So, as the plane took off, he immediately held Neha's hands out of nervousness.

"What the hell are you doing?" Neha yelled as she pulled her hands back. She didn't like Akash's behaviour. So, Akash had to control his nervousness throughout the flight. Then, by evening they had reached Kochi.

Akash and Neha had a good honeymoon trip. They had enjoyed a lot on the beaches of Kochi, waterfalls of Munnar hill-station, tea gardens of Thekkady, and boat-house at back-waters of Kumarakom. They had some quarrels over there, but at the same time enjoyed a lot. Then, after a week, they had landed Mumbai.

While Akash and Neha were in the bus towards Dhran, Neha said, "Akash, once we reach Dhran, we should plan a baby."

"Okay." Akash said dumbly. But Neha gave a weird expression to him. She was expecting him to ask the reason. "What happened?"

"Why are you so dumb? I told you about the baby and you just agreed." Neha said. "Do you really have any idea about having a baby and bringing it up?"

"Now what's wrong? You said, so I agreed." Akash said. "We are married now. So, some day or the other, we are going to have a baby."

"What do you know about having a child?" Neha asked, but Akash just gave a blank look. "We have to plan for its future, education, and much more."

"Okay." Akash said while trying to understand what Neha meant.

"Firstly, we are twenty-four right now. If we plan a baby now, then we will be around twenty-five when it's born. So, when we will be sixty, our child will be thirty-five. At that age, it will be settled and we will be able to retire happily. Secondly, our parents are healthy right now. So, they can take care of the child, if we happen to go somewhere for a couple of days. Thirdly, by the time we are thirty, our child will be old enough to travel with us anywhere we want. Fourthly, you are still struggling with your book. So, by the time your book is launched, our child will be old enough. Then, I can start my own business. Fifthly, the education and medical facilities are getting costlier day-by-day. So, the sooner we plan, the better it will be." Neha said. But Akash was just staring at her, wondering who was giving her that knowledge. But, he found logical and so, he agreed.

Even though Neha didn't like Akash, she had a good patch-up with Pratima and Prashant. They had a better understanding for each other. They were not in-laws to each other but good friends.

Next day, Akash and Neha had reached Dhran. After reaching home, Neha furtively got ready and straight away went to the kitchen to help Pratima.

"Why are you down so early?" Pratima asked. "Take some rest beta."

"It's okay maa." Neha said and started her work.

"And what about your swimming and tennis practice? I hope you are continuing." Pratima said.

"Actually maa, I and Akash are planning to have a baby first. Then, we will do the rest." Neha said.

"Oh! That's great." Pratima said happily. Then, Prashant and Akash came for the breakfast and their day began.

During the day, Neha had received a phone call. It was her friend Hansika's call. "I am not talking to you." She said as she picked the call.

"Hey, I am sorry. I had told you I had a family function to attend during your wedding." Hansika said. "That's why I am planning to visit you this weekend. And can I come to your place?"

"Yes of course, you can." Neha said. Then they continued their chat for a while before ending the call. In the evening, Neha had informed Akash, Pratima, and Prashant about Hansika.

Then, Friday had arrived. Akash had reached Sardar Patel chowk to receive Hansika. He saw a bus arriving from the far end. The bus reached and halted over there. Akash saw some passengers climbing down. Then, he saw a beautiful girl climbing down the bus.

Akash was stunned on seeing that girl. He hadn't seen such a beautiful girl in his life time. Then, the girl took out her phone and dialed a number. But to Akash's surprise, his own phone rang. He saw that is was Hansika's call. He had realised that the girl was Hansika.

"Hello." Akash said.

"Akash, I have reached here." Hansika said.

"I guess, I have seen you." Akash said. Hansika turned around and saw Akash waiving his hands towards her. So, she moved towards him.

"Hi." Hansika said with a smile which amazed Akash.

"Hello." Akash replied with the same smile. He placed her bag on the deck to help her. Then, she sat behind him and they moved on.

Akash had never imagined such a beautiful girl would accompany him on a ride someday. It was a fantasy for him. "I hope your journey was good." He said.

"Yeah, it was good." Hansika replied. "By the way, how is Neha and everyone at home?"

"Everyone is fine. Neha is waiting for you desperately." Akash was enjoying a lot talking to Hansika. Though he didn't loved her, but still he was attracted towards her. He was finding ways to talk to her. He wanted to take a longer route, but he was getting late for his shop. Then, they had reached home.

Neha was already waiting for Hansika outside. "Hey, hi!" she said while hugging her. Even Hansika was too excited to meet her. Then, Neha led her towards the guest bedroom while Akash carried her bag inside.

Hansika had a good time with Akash's family on the breakfast table. She had made a good patch-up with them because of her jolly, talkative, and energetic nature.

Neha saw that Akash was again and again staring at Hansika. So, she made a sharp glare at him which Akash understood at once.

After the breakfast, Prashant and Akash had left for the shop. Hansika, spent her day along with Neha and Pratima. In the evening, they had also visited Neha's parents' house.

In the evening, when everyone was there on the dining table, Hansika asked, "Akash what book are you writing?"

"Ah! Actually it's a fiction-fantasy story based in medieval period." Akash said.

"Oh! That's great." Hansika said. "Neha told me about your book."

"By the way Akash, Hansika has also written a novel of the same genre." Neha said. "She has brought a copy for us. It's the best seller on Amazon."

"Oh! It is?" Akash was startled.

"Congratulations. That's really great." Pratima said as she and Prashant too were amazed.

"By the way Hansika, what is your qualification?" Prashant asked.

"Uncle, I have done B.A. in history." Hansika said.

"Oh, so you like history." Prashant said.

"Yeah, Indian history is my favourite." Hansika said. "That's why my novel is based on medieval period." Akash was startled hearing that. He had same likes just that of Hansika.

After the dinner and the kitchen chores, Hansika was in the living room along with Neha and Pratima watching their favourite movie. At that time, Akash was in his bedroom, going through Hansika's novel. It had a beautiful cover-page of a throne and below it was written 'HANSIKA GALANI'. After reading Hansika's name, Akash guessed how proud she must have felt. Then, he started reading the book.

While reading, Akash wondered why he was so slow. He was good only in writing, but in that too he was far behind. 'I wish I could rewind the time' – he always told himself and this time again he said, so that he would take himself to the time when he was sixteen years old. He would take admission along with Hansika, befriend her, and complete his book along with her.

It was bed-time. Neha entered the bedroom and saw Hansika's novel in Akash's hands. "By the way, why were you staring at Hansika again and again?" Neha teased him, but he just gave a baffled look. "Stop pretending to be unknown. I know what's going on in your mind regarding Hansika."

"What non-sense." Akash said while placing the book on his side table.

"Akash, don't try to play with me. I know how men's brain works. I have seen my brothers' having crush on some other girls." Neha said while readying the bed.

"Did your brothers told you about their crushes?" Akash asked as he was amazed to hear about his brother-in-laws.

"No, by bhabis did." Neha said. "But the thing is, you are liking some girl is not a problem. Every men are the same. But you focusing on a girl instead of your career is the main problem. So, focus on your book first, and then on girls." Akash didn't have any other option except for agreeing with her.

Neha, Akash, and Hansika enjoyed a lot for the next couple of days. They had gone for dinner and a movie on Saturday and Sunday respectively.

Then, Hansika was returning back to Mumbai on Sunday. Neha and Akash had dropped her on the bus stop. Akash had completely read Hansika's novel and he told her that he liked it a lot.

"Please share me your photo holding my book along with your review." Hansika said to which Akash and Neha agreed. Then, it was time for the bus to depart. So, Hansika said her good byes and left.

CHAPTER ELEVEN

Akash and Neha would always get up at six o'clock in the morning. They both would get ready and have breakfast together. Then as usual, Akash would start writing his novel and Neha would continue her kitchen work along with Pratima. After that, Akash would go to his shop along with Prashant and return back at eight o'clock in the evening. Neha would wait for Akash the whole day as a newlywed wife would do. But after the dinner, Akash would again sit with his book.

Even on the Sundays, Akash would spend his time with his book. Neha always expected him to take her to dinner or some outing, atleast once a week. But she didn't want to disturb him. She knew that someday, Akash would be a successful writer. After the dinner, she would complete the kitchen chores and stay with Pratima and Prashant in the living room watching their favourite television show. Then by ten o'clock, she would enter her bedroom.

Then after around fifteen days, a new chapter of Akash's and Neha's life was about to start. It was a Monday morning when Akash was getting ready to leave for his shop. Neha had missed her periods. She had a doubt that she was pregnant. So, after a couple of days' test, she had confirmed that she was pregnant.

Neha got too excited after realizing the news. She couldn't believe her eyes. So, she immediately heralded

Akash. "There is a good news." She said excitedly.

"Is it?" Akash understood her words. Even he couldn't believe at first. So, he excitedly hugged her and said, "Oh Neha, thank you so much for this gift." Then they both went down to herald Prashant and Pratima at the breakfast table.

"Don't get too excited, both of you. First we should go to the gynecologist and confirm the news." Pratima said and so everyone agreed. During the day time, Pratima had taken Neha to the gynecologist and confirmed her pregnancy.

A new phase of Neha's life had begun and this time, she was expecting more time from Akash. But Akash was already stuck between shop, book, and home. And now, it was Neha's pregnancy. Most of the time, Akash would accompany Neha for regular check-ups. But there were times when Akash used to avoid and Pratima would accompany Neha.

Then, Neha's birthday was nearing. It was her first birthday after the marriage. But she didn't know whether she could expect something from Akash or not, taking her past experience into consideration. But a day prior to her birthday, when Akash was back home, he told Neha that he had planned a surprise for her. Neha was shocked to learn that. "What surprise?" she asked.

"Have patience. I will let you know tomorrow." Akash said. Then, Neha waited for the next day. But, as her birthday arrived, Akash just wished her in the morning, worked on his novel, got ready, and had his breakfast. Neha was still waiting for the surprise. Then, after breakfast, as Akash was leaving, Neha stopped him at the door. "Where is my surprise?" She asked him in a romantic way.

"You will have to wait for it till the evening." Akash said in the same romantic way and left. Neha was left startled.

What surprise it was, she wondered. But still, she waited for it.

In the evening when Akash had returned home, he saw that Neha was already in the living room waiting for him. "Where is my surprise gift?" She asked.

"I knew you would be desperate for this." Akash said while taking out a box out of his pocket and handing it to Neha. "This is for you."

"What this?" Neha asked while unwrapping the box. It was a perfume. So, this was his surprise for her first birthday after marriage. She had realized that she could expect nothing from Akash. She was deeply hurt, but had to swallow her anger. She wanted to throw the perfume bottle on Akash's face. She didn't like the gift. But as her in-laws were present, so, she had to say that it was a nice gift.

"Actually this is nothing. We are going for the dinner." Akash said excitedly. So, Neha accepted the offer half-heartedly.

While on their way towards the restaurant, Neha wanted to cry. But she had to kill her tears in her eyes. She was pregnant and it was her first birthday after marriage. She was expecting Akash to make it as the best day of her life. But he had spoiled everything. "Why are you doing this Akash?"

"I didn't get you." Akash said with a flummoxed look.

"Akash, this is my first birthday after our marriage and you are gifting me this." Neha said disappointedly. "When you said yesterday that you are having a surprise for me, I wondered you that we would be visiting some nearby out-station. But you are taking me just on a diner."

"Neha, please." Akash tried to make it clear.

"Don't worry. Today I am not going to bother you." Neha said while wiping her tears. Then, they had reached the restaurant. Over there too, Neha's mood was off. Akash tried to talk to her to convince her, but that didn't work.

Soon, Neha's sixth month had begun. Akash had just returned from his shop when Neha told him that she had an appointment with the gynecologist. But Akash refused to accompany her by saying that he had to work on his novel.

"Akash, please keep your book aside for sometime. Don't you have any responsibility towards your child?" Neha asked in anger.

"Neha, I need to complete this book as soon as possible." Akash said. He was too much worried about his book.

"But right now, I don't need your book. I need you." Neha said. "You are so much engrossed in writing that you are totally unaware about me. You don't even ask whether I am hungry or not, is my body aching, am I able to sleep or not, nothing you are worried about."

Akash realized his mistake. So, to cheer up Neha, he happily agreed and accompanied Neha. In the clinic too, Akash was just wondering about his book. Throughout the day, he already had limited time for writing, and from that too, he had to shell out some for Neha's treatment. And spending too much time on social media was also destroying him. He again wished if he could rewind his time so that he could finish his book along with Hansika and marry her.

It was the seventh month. Neha's baby shower had happened. But still Akash was totally blank about his child's future.

"Akash, have you decided anything regarding our child's future?" Neha asked while she was readying the bed. But Akash just gave a blank look. Neha understood his reply. "I guess, I have to decide by myself for our child. It's useless talking to you on this topic." Then, on next day, Neha's parents took her to their home.

Neha was staying at her parents' home for the first after marriage. She and Akash would again talk in the same way as they did before their marriage – talking at ten o'clock at night.

Then in the ninth month, the happiest day for Neha and Akash had arrived. A cute baby boy was born to Neha. As soon as they received the news, Akash and his parents rushed towards the hospital.

A new member had arrived in Akash's and Neha's family. Akash would visit Neha house twice a day to meet his baby, before and after the shop timing. So, Akash was getting tucked between his business, home, book, and baby. He would hardly get time for his book.

Soon, the name ceremony of the baby had happened. 'Baadal' was the name given to the baby.

Akash would everyday visit Neha and Baadal. Sometimes, even Pratima and Prashant would visit by bringing toys for the kid. The rest of the days, they would make a video call to Neha to see the baby.

"Akash, your boy is not letting me sleep the whole night." Neha said.

"What is his timing?" Akash asked.

"He sleeps at ten and wakes up at twelve. Then again he sleeps at three and wakes up at seven." Neha said. "By this, I am not able to sleep properly."

Akash just gave a blank look at her. He was already lacking time for his book. He was wondering what he would face after Neha's return. "Akash, you still have time. Complete your book as much as possible before my and Baadal's return."

Then after three months, Neha and Baadal were finally home. Akash and his parents were too excited for the baby's welcome. Akash had spent his day on his shop and the evening with Baadal. But the night was something unexpected.

Neha was already lying down, but Akash was still with his book. "Akash, right now please go to sleep before Baadal wakes up." Neha said. So, Akash agreed and kept his book on the side. But, as they both were about to sleep, Baadal woke up and started crying. Akash and Neha got worried. They immediately switched off the lights and started patted Baadal, trying to make him sleep. But he still crying.

"He is hungry." Neha said. So, she took Baadal in her lap and started feeding him.

Akash saw that Neha was too tired. She rested her head on the backrest of the bed to have a nap while cautiously feeding the baby. Then, after a few minutes, the baby was done. Akash saw that Baadal had completely woken up. He was fresh and didn't need to sleep while he and Neha were drowsy.

"Give him to me." Akash said. So, Neha passed Baadal to him. As Akash took Baadal in his hands, he started his mischief after seeing his father. So, even Akash started playing with him. He was trying to make him sleep while moving from one end of the room to another, while Neha was lying to get a nap. Then after sometime, Neha took the baby and allowed Akash to lie down.

"Now just imagine, how I did this for three months while you were sleeping over here." Neha taunted Akash. Then after sometime, Baadal again started crying. He wanted to sleep. So, Neha made him sleep in her lap. Even Akash lay down as he couldn't control his sleep.

Baadal was fast asleep and so was Akash. So, after placing Baadal in his cot, Neha kicked Akash hard. "Hey, what's wrong with you?" Akash asked trying to control his voice so that Baadal wouldn't get up.

"How careless you are. You couldn't even wait for me." Neha scolded him. "You were sleeping for three months. Can't you be awake for a little while?"

Akash saw that it was almost three o'clock in the morning. He didn't have the stamina to reply back. Then, Neha went to sleep and so him. But at around seven o'clock, Baadal again woke up and started crying. So, Neha too woke up to feed him. But she didn't woke up Akash as she as she thought that he had to spend his day at his shop.

This continued for almost six months till Baadal's sleeping time got fixed. But that had disturbed his sleep which ultimately had disturbed his writing schedule. Upon that, their visits to the child specialist time to time for vaccination or other treatments were also killing his time. At that time, he would think again for a time rewind so that he would make himself a successful author before his marriage.

The days went on. After giving the maximum time possible for writing his Novel, Akash was finally about to complete his story. Even a couple of weeks was remaining for Baadal's first birthday. So, Akash had kept his son's birthday as the deadline to publish his novel. Akash's Novel was going to be published soon, and he was too excited for that. Even Neha was eagerly waiting to hold her husband's novel in her hand. And then, after somedays, his story was complete.

"Finally, my story is novel is complete." Akash said happily. He had finished taking down the story into his computer in M.S. word format. He had also read the complete book to see how it felt reading it. He really enjoyed his book.

"Now how are you going to publish it?" Neha asked.

"I will search some publishers and talk to them for publishing the book." Akash said casually.

"Yeah, as if they are waiting for you." Neha teased. "Akash, be practical."

"So, what do you think I am supposed to do?" Akash asked.

"That too should I tell you? Akash, what do you know about publishing?" Neha asked.

"We go to the publisher with our story and they publish it." Akash replied randomly.

"Oh! Is it?" Neha again taunted. "But what if the publisher rejects you story?"

"Why will he reject it? It's a nice story." Akash said.

"But what if he doesn't want to publish it?" Neha asked. "Okay, just tell me how many types of publishing are there?" But Akash just gave a bemused look. "You don't have any idea, isn't it? First option is, you can self-publish you book where only you are responsible for writing, designing, printing, and marketing the book. In this, complete royalty is yours. Second option is, you hire a publisher, where he takes care of printing and designing while you are just to write and market the book. In this, you have to pay a certain amount to the publisher. Third option is called traditional publishing, where the publisher pays you a huge amount, publishes the book, and sells it."

"Okay, but from where did you get this idea?" Akash asked. He was completely unaware about those multiple options for publishing.

"Few days back, there was a free live seminar for a couple of days by a reputed publisher about publishing and marketing the book. I had come to know about it through Instagram. I had attended it." Neha said.

"Okay, so I will go with the traditional publishing." Akash said.

"Don't even think of that. Usually, only the world famous personalities go for this option. Because, the publisher is confident that his book will definitely succeed. And in your case, forget about international level, no one even knows you outside this house." Neha said. "I would suggest, you go for the self-0publishing option. But for that too, you need to create a market for your book."

"So, how am I supposed to create a market?"

"Akash, why are you so dependent?" Neha was getting bored explain Akash. "Go and find out ways to be known on a wider level." Akash was completely startled hearing that. Somehow he had managed to write the book, but now he had to find out the way to successfully publish it.

CHAPTER TWELVE

From that day onwards, Akash had started searching the publishers online. As he didn't know about self-publishing and he knew that the traditional publishing won't work in his case, he choose the second option. He searched all the publishers online, read about them, and tried contacting them. He even got the itineraries of all the publishers.

"I am going for the paid option." Akash said to Neha.

"But just don't trust anyone blindly. Read all the terms and conditions carefully and then sign the contract. Even just don't choose the package in a hurry. First talk to maa and papa and then decide." Neha said to which Akash agreed.

It was a fine Sunday, so everyone was at home. Akash immediately went down to talk to his parents about publishing his book. But they were too totally blank about it. "Akash, first show us your manuscript. Let us read it first and then carry forward." Pratima said.

"Yeah, but the publisher will do the editing work. I just need to finalise the package and pay him first." Akash said.

"First let me talk to him." Prashant said. But that was Sunday, so they postponed it to the next day.

Next morning, Akash felt like as if he was having ample of time. He was done with his book and so, he was free. he got up on his usual time, got ready, and started playing with Baadal before the breakfast. After a long time, he was having a good time with his child. Then everyone had their breakfast and Akash and Prashant went to their shop.

Akash was too excited to publush his book. He again reminded Prashant about talking to the publisher. "Akaish, wait for some time. Let me complete this work. Then, I will talk to him." Prashant said.

Then, it was late afternoon. Prashant was finally free. So, he told Akash to dial the publisher's number and first talk to him. Akash was too nervous to talk to the publisher. He hadn't talked to someone regarding such a big deal. So, he just dialed the number and randomly started talking to him, "Hello, I want to publish my book."

"Wait, what are you doing?" Prashant aksed while giving a bemused look. "Let me talk."

Prashant took the phone and had a talk to the publisher. As he was a business man, he knew how to handle those types of deal. He had the best talk with the publisher. He took out all the information regarding publishing, printing, marketing, advertisements, payment, and much more

"This is how you are supposed to talk. Akash, its been years for you since you are here, and still you are unaware about handling the deals." Prashant said while handling his phone back. "Now let me talk to the other publishers." So, Akash dialed the other publisher's number and again Prashant had the same talk with him. One-by-one, he had talked to around six-to-seven publishers and had finalized one of them, which he thaoght suited Akash's requirements.

The next day had arrived. On the breakfast table, Prashant said to Akash, "Today, you again talk to the publisher which we selected yesterday. I want you to talk because its you who needs to understand the procedure. Firstr ask him about the payment's method. After its done, talk to him about your book, and how much time it will take to get published. If you still don't understand, then klet me know."

'Okay papa." Akash said.

It was again late afternoon when Akash and Prashant were almost free from the customers. So, Akash dialed the publisher's number and again had a talk with him about what Prashant had told him. The publisher had send him the bank details on his email. Akash checked his email and then made the required payment of eighty thousand in one go. Then he started receiving the other emails like, confirmation mails, further procedures, and everything which was required.

Akash was a bit relaxed. But Neha wasn't. "Akash, you novel's journey hasn't ended. It has started from now. Dint just depend on the publisher for your marketing. You too do something."

"But the package already includes media and social media advertisements. Just relax." Akash said.

"But it's not going to harm you if you make some efforts from your side. It's just going to help you." Neha tried to convience him. But Akash seemed to be of tough hide.

Then, Akash's most avaited day had arrived. It was again a fine Sunday morning when suddenly the door-bell rang. Akash went to open the door and saw that someone had send a parcel to him. He read his name and address on it. But, at first, he didn't understand who had send what. He signed on the paper and took the parcel. It was a huge box.

"What's it, Akash?" Pratima asked as she saw the box in his hand.

"The publisher has send something." Akash said after reading the sender's name. he had understood that it was regarding his book. so, he immediately opened the box and found that it had his author copies.

"Oh, these are my books." Akash said excitedly. Even Neha and Prashant came out as they heared Akash.

"Oh my God." Pratima said excitedly.

"Show me." Neha said. she too was excited.

"Congratulation son." Prashant said as he happily kissed Akash's forehead.

Akash was holding his book with his name on it. It was his story which he was holding. He couldn't believe his eyes. He was so deeply moved that he was again and again surfing the book. He gifted the first book to his parents and kept one for himself.

"Now what are you going to do with these books?" Pratima asked.

"Sell it in discounted rates." Neha suggested. "By this, you will get more publicity." Everyone liked Neha's idea and so, they agreed.

That day, the first thing Akash and Neha did was to post the pictures of the novel on their social media page. Form them, social media was the only socurce for edvertising the book. Then, Akash took one of his books and started reading it.

Before reading the book, Akash was continuously glaring at the cover page having his name below the title. The feeling which he was getting after holding his book didn't have any words to describe. Then, he started reading the book.

Akash had started reading the book from the first page including acknowledgement, introductions, index, and everything which usually people avoid. But it was written by him. So, he was enjoying it a lot. Then his story began.

Neha saw that Akash was just going on reading his book and avoiding everything else, including her and Baadal.

"Akash, you have already spend a lot of time after writing. Atleast now you spend your time with us. Even Baadal needs your time. He is already a year old. You have to play with him, take him out for a ride, or anything else to develop his bonding with you."

"Neha, I was waiting for this since long. Just give me a day. By tomorrow, I am just yours and Baadal's." Akash said and started reading his book.

"Huh. You are assuming that your work for this book is done. But you still have a long way dear." Neha said and left the room. But still Akash was just with his book.

Akash was reading the story from the readers' point of view. He was so engrossed in the story that he was completely unaware about anything else. He was in love with the story very much. He just took two brakes for lunch and dinner. Then, by ten o'clock at night, he was done.

"Now finally, I am satisfied." Akash said as he took a sigh of relief. By that time, Baadal was already asleep.

"I have got some messages. Some of my friends want to buy your book." Neha said.

"Oh, is it?" Akash asked excitedly. "Let me too check my messages."

"Didn't you use your social media today?" Neha was startled as Akash was social media addicted. But that day, he didn't check it as he was so engrossed in reading his book.

Akash had started distributed all of his books to the ones who had ordered it. One he had reserved for his parents, one for himself and Neha, one for His in-laws, and one for Tejas. He was too happy on seeing his author copies being sold. Even all of his friends and relatives had bought it and gave their reviews.

The days went on. Akash was already done with his author copies. But as he checked his author dashboard, the sales were none. He always followed up the publisher regarding the sale. But the publisher just replied by saying that they would update his dashboard everytime the sale would happen.

"Akash, I had told you earlier. I needed to have some marketing strategies for your book. It's your first book and no one knows you as an author. First you should have created your identity." Neha said while they were on their dinner table.

"Even when you had started writing, I had warned you regarding this. You were so engrossed in writing that you were completely cut-off from the outer world. Son, you have be social to sell something." Prashant said.

"You should do one thing. Go and visit the publisher personally and talk to him about what are you supposed to do now." Pratima said and so, Akash agreed.

Next day, Akash had left for Mumbai to meet the publisher. He was too nervous. He hadn't talked to someone regarding such a big topic in earnest. He wanted to ask Prashant whether he could accompany him. But Prashant wanted him to grow now. He couldn't spoon-feed his son everytime.

Prashant and Pratima were too worried about their son. Even Neha was worried. She just prayed that he would succeed this time when he left.

Next day, Akash was in Mumbai. He had reached the publisher's office by ten o'clock. Over there, after waiting for around half an hour, he met the man who was in touch with him throughout his publication journey. His name was Aditya.

"Aditya, what is the update regarding my novel?" Akash asked.

"Sir everything is already updated on your dashboard. Nothing is remaining." Aditya confirmed after checking his dashboard.

"But what about the sales?" Akash asked.

"Sir, we can't force anyone to buy your book. It completely depends on the readers whether they will like your story or not. Our job is just to make the book available in the market." Aditya said.

"But how are we supposed to promote it?" Akash asked.

"Sir, we are trying our level best to promote it from our side. We have also made your social media pages for the promotion from your side. You just keep on updating your page and try to reach out maximum people out there." Aditya said. "We also have given you posters. You can distribute it in the malls, book stores, colleges, libraries, and other public places."

The publisher tried to convince Akash indirectly that he didn't have proper marketing strategies. But Akash was not convinced with him. After the discussion for around half a day, he left the office. And by next morning, he was back to Dhran.

Akash had the same talk with his family what he had with the publisher. He was too depressed. He didn't have any hopes left. "Akash, if you are not satisfied, then cancel the contract." Prashant said on his breakfast table.

"But papa, we have paid eighty thousand." Akash said.

"Son, you cannot blame the publisher completely. We don't know what his fault is. But your fault is, you are not at all aware of what's going on outside the four walls of this house." Prashant said. "First make people aware about you. Then, tell them about your book."

"We can do one thing. We have posters. Atleast distribute it in the colleges, libraries, and all the public places." Neha suggested. Everyone liked her idea. So, from that day, Akash went to all the colleges along with Dhaval to distribute the posters. Most of the colleges didn't allow him, as it wasn't regarding the syllabus. But there were some who allowed. He also went to the libraries and told the managers about his book.

Akash continued to promote his book for almost a year. Baadal was two years old, but still his book was nowhere. He had even ordered more author copies and tries to sell them on discounted rates. But the people who knew him had already bought the books, and the people who didn't know him weren't interested. In-fact people of Dhran weren't interested in reading, and Akash was unable to reach outside the town. He even gave the books as a complimentary to his customers who would bulk order oil paints from him. He would request them to give their reviews on his novel. But the customers were startled to see such a huge novel. They hesitated to read, as they weren't good readers. They just congratulated him, took pictures with him holding the book, and moved on.

Akash was deeply hurt on seeing his book neglected by everyone. He had spent years for writing it and a couple of years for promoting it. His hard-work was seen going in vein. He was a good writer, but not a good seller.

"Akash, your book is not getting sold. Its better you cancel your contract with the publisher, improve it, and again publish it with some other good publisher." Neha said during the dinner. So, he agreed. After the dinner, he straight away went to his bedroom, started his computer, and sent an email to the publisher regarding cancelation of the contract. He didn't want to so that. But he had to.

His heart was too heavy to accept that. It seemed that his writing career was ending.

Akash was on his terrace, wondering why that was happening to him. He couldn't be good at anything, be it studies, business, family, friends, or writing. He was holding his book in his hands and crying. He didn't want to end his book that way. He was crying harder. At that time, he prayed to God deeply to rewind his time. He prayed harder. He wished to go back in time when his S.S.C. exams were over, so that he would make good decisions regarding his career. He wished to go back in time, so that he would make good friends and contacts with other people. He wished to go back in time, so that he would develop himself in each and every field. He wished to go back in time, so that he would do a course of his choice and be an author at early age. He wished "If I could rewind the time."

CHAPTER THIRTEEN

'Tik – tik'. The morning alarm rang. Akash got awaken but was still sleepy. He groped his hand towards his mobile phone on his bedside table to put off the alarm while his head was still under the pillow. But he couldn't find the mobile phone. Even the alarm wasn't familiar.

"Akash, wake up." Pratima called from downstairs. "It's seven o'clock. Now as your S.S.C. exams are over, that does not mean you are supposed to lie down the whole day."

"S.S.C. exams!" Akash wondered. He was already married and was having a kid. So why was Pratima talking about S.S.C. He moved the pillow from his head and was completely startled to see the room in which he was. It wasn't his bedroom. "Neha." He called but there was no answer. Oh wait! He remembered that it was his own bedroom. But why the interior arrangement were like that which were there around ten years back, he didn't understand. His father had renovated the whole house just before his marriage. He got up and even found himself in the clothes which he had around ten years back. Then, he looked into the mirror and saw that he was much younger. He didn't understand what was going on. He walked towards the wall calendar and saw the date – 20th March 2006. It was the first day of his three months long holiday which he had after his S.S.C. exams. Oh! His time had rewind. "My time has rewind!" He said to himself excitedly.

"Akash, are you coming to have your breakfast or not?" Pratima called.

"Yes maa." Akash replied.

Akash furtively got ready and went down to have his breakfast. Over there, he saw that his parents were already on the dining table. He felt too happy on seeing the younger version of his parents. "Good morning maa, good morning papa." Akash said while touching their feet. His parents were shocked.

"Have your breakfast." Pratima said while passing the plate having tow freshly cooked chapattis with butter and jam on it.

"Maa, can I bring Misal-pav from Jalaram restaurant?" Akash asked. But his parents were again shocked to know that he knew about Jalaram's Misal-pav at that age.

"And who is going to have these chapattis?" Pratima asked.

"It's okay Pratima. Let him have what he wants." Prashant said.

"Thank you." Akash said and so, he immediately moved out. But Prashant stopped him. "Take the money." So, Akash remembered that he didn't have his own money now. He had to borrow from his parents just like earlier.

"Akash I wanted to talk to you." Prashant said while giving him the money. "Have you decided anything regarding your career?

"Yes papa, I want to study history and literature." Akash replied confidently.

"History and literature!" Prashant was shocked. Even Pratima wondered what he was saying.

"But why history and literature?" Pratima asked.

"Actually maa, I love history and I want to be an author." Akash said. So, Prashant and Pratima exchanged glowers in amazement.

"Beta, take your time and decide. Don't be in a hurry." Prashant said. Then, he was about to leave when Akash interrupted, "Papa, can I join gym from tomorrow?"

"Yes, sure. Do your admission over there today itself and pay whatever the fee is." Prashant said and left for his shop. Then, even Akash went to buy Misal-pav and then, he went to the gym.

After the breakfast, Akash went out to be with his friends. While playing badminton, Nitya asked everyone, "What are you all planning regarding your career?"

"I am taking admission in commerce." Dhaval said while hitting the shuttle cork towards Sejal.

"What are you planning?" Manish asked Nitya.

"I will be doing B.D.S." Nitya replied. "What about you all?"

"I am going for science. After that, I will be doing engineering." Dhruv said.

"Me too." Rohan said.

"Even me." Manish added. Akash was staring at them. He was wordless.

"What kind of hobbies you all are having?" Akash asked.

"I just like watching movies." Ankita said bluntly.

"My hobby is to sleep or play the whole day." Dhaval said. "But why are you asking this?"

"Why don't you all make your career out of your hobbies?" Akash asked confidently. But everyone just gave a silent answer.

"I don't think career and hobbies depend on each other." Sejal said in her soft voice. Everyone turned towards her to listen. "I mean, career is something by which you can please others like your family, your boss or your clients and customers. But hobbies are something which you do for yourself."

"It's not necessary. What if someone's hobby is singing? He or she can make a good career out of it." Ankita said.

"By the way Akash, what are your hobbies?" Minakshi asked.

"I am having interest in history and writing." Akash said.

"History and writing!" Ankita was startled. "How many books have you read?"

"None. But I know I can make a good career out of it." Akash said confidently. He knew what his future was. He wanted to tell everyone about his time rewind, but he opted to be silent as none would believe him. "By the way, I am joining the gym from tomorrow. Is anyone interested to accompany me?"

"What is the time for your gym?" Dhaval asked.

"Five o'clock to seven o'clock in the morning." Akash replied.

"No ways. I won't be able to get-up so early." Dhaval said.

The summer afternoon was making them sweat. "It's getting too hot. Let's meet in the evening." Nitya said and so, everyone moved towards their home.

As Akash reached home, he lay on the sofa and switched on the television when his younger brother Tejas was back to home from school.

"How was your exam?" Pratima asked while arranging the plates on the dining table.

"It was excellent, maa." Tejas replied happily as he tossed his bag on the sofa. Akash knew his brother Tejas was talented as compared to him, though he was three years younger to him. He was not surprised to know that his brother's exam was excellent.

"The lunch is ready. Both of you get fresh and come fast." Pratima called.

Akash, Tejas and Pratima were having lunch when Tejas said, "Maa, after my tuition classes, my friends will be coming over here for studies. We have got some previous years' question papers to solve."

"That's nice." Pratima said while pouring some rice in his plate.

"Maa, will you please check our answer sheets?" Tejas asked while having his bite.

"But why don't you do it by yourself?" Pratima asked.

"We don't want to waste time in that." Tejas said.

"But you should check your sheets yourself. By this, you will get to know what mistakes you have done." Pratima said. Akash wasn't shocked to hear all that. He knew his brother was studious. He was happy for him. Then, Tejas left.

"All the best." Akash wished Tejas. Then, after the lunch, he asked Pratima, "Maa, can I go to Mumbai and buy some fiction-fantasy novels?"

"Akash, what's happened to you? Why are you into reading and writing so much? I mean, reading is good for you, but you weren't like this earlier." Pratima said. "But still, you can go. I will talk to your Mansi maasi."

After the lunch, Akash straight away went to his bedroom, switched on his computer, and started searching about Harry Potter and The Lord of the Rings' novels. He didn't have any mode for online purchase, so he just saw the images and switched off the computer. Then he took one of his rough books which had some empty pages. He started writing the outline of his novel.

Akash was too much excited about his time rewind. He knew what he would face in his near future, what interest he would develop within himself, how he has to develop contacts, and how he is supposed to move forward in his life. He had no fear, but only excitement for his new life. He was very much thankful to God for fulfilling his desire.

Akash already knew the story about the novel which he had written. So, developing the outline just took some minutes for him. Then, he went down to Pratima's bedroom to get a fresh diary for his new book. Pratima saw him taking the diary, but she didn't bother about asking, thinking that he must be needing for some other work.

Akash was again and again staring at the calendar. He still couldn't believe that time had taken him eleven years back. Eleven years was a good time for him. He had an ample of time to develop his career, while his friends and classmates were just bothered about getting admission in junior colleges.

Akash had started writing his novel. His outline was completed and the chapters were also ready. Then, he went on writing his story.

In the evening, Tejas was back to home along with his friends. They entered Akash's and Tejas' room, sat on the floor, and distributed the copies of the previous years' question papers. Akash knew each and every-one of them. He even knew that they would be solving their question papers. He didn't want to disturb them. So, he went down towards the hall to watch his favourite television show, showing the story of the king of Delhi – Prithviraj Chauhan as he was a history lover. Afterwards, as the show was over, he went out to join his colony friends.

It was eight o'clock in the evening, when Prashant returned home from his shop. "Where are the children?" He asked Pratima.

"Tejas is along with his friends in his bedroom, preparing for tomorrow and Akash is with his friends outside." Pratima said.

"Did he decide anything?" Prashant asked.

"Prashant, I guess he wants to go with history and writing." Pratima said.

"Pratima, does he have any idea about reading and writing?" Prashant asked. "It's regarding his whole career. Okay, call him. I want to talk to him." So, Pratima went out to call Akash.

"Did you call me, papa?" Akash asked as soon as he entered the house.

"Yes I called you. Sit." Prashant said and so, Akash sat near him. He was a bit uncomfortable. He thought his father would ask him about his future plans.

"What happened?" He asked nervously.

"Will you join M.S.-C.I.T. classes?" Prashant asked.

"Papa, I don't want to join any classes in this vacation. In-fact, I was about to ask you about going to Mumbai to buy some fiction- fantasy novels." Akash said.

"Akash, I am not saying that you don't go for writing. It's a good field. But what do you know about it?" Prashant asked. "I was thinking that you should go for Architecture."

"No papa." Akash replied bluntly. "The only things I am good at are history and writing. Please give me one chance to prove."

Prashant and Pratima exchanged looks with each other, guessing what was going inside Akash's mind. "Okay, I will give you one chance. But just be careful, beta. You are deciding regarding your career." Prashant said. "You can go to Mumbai tomorrow and get your books."

"Thank you papa." Akash said happily. Then, even Tejas' friends came down. Prashant and Pratima wished them and then, they went.

While lying in the bed, Akash was just wondering how his life would be once he would become a successful author at an early age. He was missing Neha a lot at that time. He knew where she stayed but it was useless visiting her. She wouldn't recognize him. He was too excited to take admission in Hansika's college, so that he would be with her throughout his writing journey. He was too excited to go to Mumbai and buy the novels. Then, he switched off the lights and went to sleep.

CHAPTER FOURTEEN

Akash had made up his mind to be an author. He was firm on his decision. So, the next day, he was ready to leave for Mumbai along with Tejas and Pratima. Tejas' exams were over and he wanted to accompany his brother and mother.

In the evening, Prashant dropped Akash, Pratima, and Tejas at the bus stop. "Take care of yourself and the kids and call me once you reach home in the morning," Prashant said to Pratima.

"Even you take care and call me once you reach home," Pratima said. Then, the bus arrived. Prashant showed the ticket to the conductor and so, the conductor let Akash, Pratima, and Tejas in. They said their goodbyes to Prashant and entered the bus. But, as they entered the bus, Tejas and Pratima were shocked to see the luxurious interior of the bus. "Who! Is this really a bus?" Tejas asked out of shock. They were traveling for the first in a sleeper coach bus. But Akash had seen all that stuff in his original time. So, it didn't bother him. Then, they had their berth.

The next day, Akash, Pratima, and Tejas reached Mumbai. Then, they hired a taxi and safely reached Mansi's house.

Akash, Pratima, and Tejas were always amazed to see the society where Mansi stayed. It was a luxurious sea-facing society. They entered the society and had reached Mansi's flat on the twenty-fifth floor.

"Good morning, all of you." Mansi wished them as they entered. She was a beefy women with trimmed hair. Though she was Pratima's elder sister, she hardly looked like her.

"Good morning, didi," Pratima said while hugging her.

"Good morning, maasi." Akash and Tejas said while touching her feet. "How are you?"

"I am good," Mansi said. "You all can go to Sarthak's room and lie down for a while."

"But won't he get disturbed?" Pratima asked.

"He is already in my room," Mansi said. So, they went to Sarthak's room, kept their luggage over there, and went to take a nap for a while.

Pratima, Akash, and Tejas had a good sleep for a couple of hours. Then, they woke up as they heard the knock on the door. "Pratima, the breakfast is ready," Mansi called.

"We will be there within a couple of minutes, didi," Pratima said. Then, the trio got ready and reached the dining table.

"Good morning everyone," Sarthak said as he came out of his parents' room. Sarthak was Mansi's only son who was a year older to Akash.

"Oh my God! You have grown so tall," Pratima was astonished to see Sarthak as a tall grown-up handsome guy, as she was meeting him after a long time. Even Tejas was shocked to see him but Akash just pretended to be shocked. "How are you?" Pratima added.

"I am good maasi. You say." Sarthak said while touching her feet.

"All good," Pratima replied. Then, she went to the kitchen to help Mansi while Akash, Tejas, and Sarthak had their seats. Then, Mansi's husband Saurabh came out.

"Good morning," Saurabh said. Saurabh was unlike Mansi. He was a handsome middle-aged man with a fair complexion who took good care of his health.

"Good morning maasa," Akash and Tejas said while getting up and touching his feet.

"Hey, that's okay," Saurabh said while blessing him and helping them lift up.

"So, what's your plan for today?" Saurabh asked.

"I am planning to visit some bookstores to buy some novels," Akash said.

"Then, you should go to Words' world. It's a huge store and it's the closest one." Sarthak said. "What kind of novels do you want?"

"I want to buy the Harry Potter series and The Lord of the Rings series," Akash replied.

"You should have told me. I would have sent it to you through courier." Saurabh said. "Anyways." Then, Mansi and Pratima brought the breakfast to the table.

"Sarthak is planning to go to the North-east for his summer camp. So, will you be able to send Akash and Tejas with him?" Saurabh asked Pratima. But Pratima just gave a guess and said, "I will have to ask Prashant for that."

"Then ask right now. Because their dates are from first of April to fifteenth of April. The bookings are already done. But I can talk to the camp operator to arrange the tickets for them. The fee is seven thousand rupees per person." Saurabh said.

"Wait, I will call right now," Pratima said and made a call to Prashant.

"Yes Pratima," Prashant said.

"Prashant, Jiju is saying that Sarthak is going to a summer camp in the North-East from the first of April to the fifteenth of April. So, he is asking whether we can send

Akash and Tejas or not. The fee is seven thousand rupees for one person." Pratima said.

"If it's possible on this end moment, then go for it. I will transfer the amount to Jiju's account right now." Prashant said.

"Okay," Pratima said and ended the call. Then, she turned to Saurabh and said, "He said yes."

"Then, I will do their registration by today," Saurabh said.

Then, by ten o'clock, Akash, Pratima, and Tejas had left for the store. It was on the same road, with just ten minutes walking distance. Then, they had reached the store.

As Akash, Pratima, and Tejas entered the store, they were completely startled. They were seeing such a giant luxurious store with thousands of books arranged on the shelves for the first time. It was the heaven for a books-lovers. Three of them were searching the books on the shelves. But even after several attempts, they couldn't find it. Then, Pratima had to ask one of the employees over there, who guided them towards the shelves. Akash had got his desired novel series. But, as Pratima saw the price on it, she asked Akash, "Are you seriously going to read all these books?"

"Yes maa," Akash replied. So, Pratima took the books to the counter and paid for them.

"Akash, these books are too costly. If I find that you aren't reading these books, then be ready to face the outcome." Pratima warned.

"Maa, don't worry. That won't happen." Akash confirmed. Then, they reached home. But as soon as they reached home, Akash unwrapped the book's box and started reading the first book.

"Do you read all these books?" Saurabh asked as he saw Akash with those books. Even Tejas was going through the other books.

"I haven't read them, but wanted to read them for a long," Akash said.

"By the way, yours and Tejas' admission is confirmed for the summer camp," Sarthak said.

Then, after lunchtime, Akash was again with his books while Tejas and Saurabh were busy watching their favourite movie.

Akash was too engrossed in reading the books. He was reading the first book of one of the series. He was so deeply submerged into reading, that he wasn't aware at all about the passing time. Then, suddenly it was evening. Akash had finished reading most of the pages. Then, they had left for Dhran at Night by the same bus.

Next day, Akash, Pratima, and Tejas were back home. As Akash was already late that day, he had missed the gym. So, he immediately got ready and went to have his breakfast.

After the breakfast, Akash and Tejas had gone out to be with their friends. Akash could have chosen to sit with the novels which he had bought, but he remembered what the reason for his book's failure was in his original time. It was due to lack of socializing of himself. And as now, he had got a second chance, he didn't want to continue the same mistake.

Akash spend a good time with his friends, playing badminton, then Ludo, then Changas, and much more. Then, by afternoon he was back home for the lunch. It was only after the lunch that he sat with his novels.

Akash remembered that he needed to note down all the difficult words' meanings so that he could use them in his own novel. So, he again he brought one more diary of

Prashant and divided it alphabet wise.

Akash was used to that type of language in those novels, since his original time. But still he noted down the difficult words along with their meanings. He knew that he had ample of time for that. Then, by evening, he was again with his friends.

On the thirty-first of March, Akash and Tejas were ready to leave for Mumbai. Pratima had accompanied them to Mumbai. Like last time, Prashant had dropped them on the bus stop. Then, as the bus arrived and they climbed in and had their berths. By next morning, they had reached Mumbai at Mansi's place.

"Good morning," Mansi said.

"Good morning didi," Pratima replied as she tugged the luggage inside.

"All set?" Mansi asked.

"Yeah," Pratima said. "Shall we move to Sarthak's room?"

"Yes," Mansi replied. Then, they had a nap for a couple of hours over there. In the afternoon, they had their train to New Delhi.

Akash, Tejas, Pratima, Sarthak, and Mansi reached Mumbai Central Railway Station. As they reached the station, they saw that the Rajdhani Express was already there waiting for its departure on the first platform. "The train had already arrived. Hurry up." Mansi said. But due to her heavy body, she couldn't run. So, Pratima tried to be with her. "You go with the children. I will come slowly." She said to Pratima.

"Okay," Pratima said. "Children, hurry up." She said and so they hurried towards the platform. Then, they had reached the platform. Over there, many of their colleagues had already reached before time. Akash saw the Rajdhani

Express for the first time. He was too impressed to see such a luxurious train. "Wow!" He exclaimed.

"Bro, this is still nothing. You see it from inside." Sarthak said.

"Which one is your carriage? Do you have the seat numbers?" Pratima asked Sarthak.

"I guess, the tour operator has all the details," Sarthak said.

"Hey, Sarthak." Sarthak heard someone calling his name. So, he turned around and saw his friends reaching him.

"Hey guys, how's everyone?" Sarthak asked.

"Have you come alone?" One of Sarthak's friends asked. So, he pointed toward Akash and Tejas and introduced them to his friends. "Guys, these are my cousins – Akash and Tejas."

"Hello." Akash wished them.

"Akash and Tejas, these are my friends – Sneha, Bhushan, Sahil, Sakshi, and Preeti." Sarthak introduced his friends to Akash and Tejas. Pratima was just looking at Sarthak's friends and wondering about who Akash and Tejas would mix up with them. Soon, Mansi had also reached the platform. Then, their tour operators also arrived. "Everyone for the Adventurous summer camp, please come over here." One of the tour operators announced. So, everyone including the parents surrounded them. "We all are in just one carriage. We will call out your name and you just have to sign on his attendance form and note down your seat number." The tour operator announced. Then, they started calling the students by their names one by one and gave them their seat numbers. Even Akash, Tejas, Sarthak, and his friends got their seat numbers. Then they were told to get inside the train as it was already time. So, Akash, Tejas, and Sarthak said their goodbyes to their mothers and entered the train. Then, their journey began.

Akash was too excited about the summer camp. He was visiting the northeast for the first time. Even he was traveling in such a luxurious train for the first time. They had arranged all their luggage and then, had their seats. All of Sarthak's friends were in the same compartment along with Tejas and Akash.

Akash was confident on being with new people around. He easily befriended them. But he saw that Tejas was a bit nervous with new people around. "What happened?" Akash muttered in his ears.

"Nothing." Tejas replied in the same low voice.

"Is everything okay?" Sakshi asked. She was just sitting opposite to Akash and had realised that Tejas was a bit uncomfortable.

"He is just worried a bit about the camp. That's all." Akash said.

"Don't worry dude. It's the first time for us too. And we are going to enjoy." Bhushan said. That made Tejas feel a bit better. Then, to make him more comfortable, Akash included him in all the talks which he had with everyone. Then soon, everyone had started talking to Tejas in a friendly manner, and so he felt confident.

Akash's train journey to New Delhi was very exciting. Though his childhood friend circle was awesome, he still needed to make more friends. He wanted to use each and every moment of his time rewind. They played, chatted, laughed, ate, and did all sorts of fun. And for that, there was no one to stop them. Even their camp colleagues from other compartments had joined them in their fun.

On next morning, they had reached New Delhi. Akash was a history fan, so he was too excited for touring the whole of Delhi. But he took care of his younger brother too. First, they went to their hotel to get fresh over there. It was a nice hotel with cozy rooms. Then, after the breakfast, they went for the sightseeing.

Akash and his camp mates toured Delhi for two days. They had gone to see Red Fort, Qutub Minar, Akshardham Mandir, Jama Masjid, Gateway of India, Rajpath, Rashtrapati bhavan, Humayun's tomb, and much more. Akash even made sure that his younger brother was enjoying the trip. They even took photographs in their digital camera for their memories. As Akash knew that in his near future, taking photos in the camera phone would become a tradition.

Then, on the next day, they had left for Darjeeling. Everyone was excited about the Himalayan trip, even Akash. On that train journey, Akash enjoyed himself with all his colleagues. Then, on the next day morning, they had reached Darjeeling.

Over there, first, they had gone to their hotels to get fresh, and then, after the breakfast they were taken to the campsite. They had to ready the tents for themselves. But again he saw Tejas nervous over there. "What happened?" Akash asked him.

"How are we going to stay in these tents?" Tejas asked nervously.

"What's the deal in that? Everyone is going to stay in their tents. And don't worry, I am there for you." Akash said. He had understood Tejas was too youngest one in the camp. So, he was a bit nervous and uncomfortable. But Akash had tried his level best to make him comfortable.

After everyone was done with their tent work, they were taken to all the nearby places. Then they had to spend the nights in their tents. It was cold over there, so they had brought their sleeping bags, jackets, and all the woolen stuff. Then, they even visited other tourist spots in Sikkim and changed their camping sites.

Then, they had gone to Meghalaya, and then to Assam. Over there too, they had a good camping. They did mountain climbing, river crossing, rafting, and all sorts of camp sports. And then, it was time to return.

Akash didn't want to return. He had enjoyed it for the first time. But he remembered that his time was rewind and so, he would get ample chances. He had made good friends on the camp. He had good memories with them. He had even exchanged his mobile number with them so that he would chat with them whenever he would get a chance.

On the train, everyone had all sorts of enjoyment again which they had done during their trip's beginning. Then, on the next day, they had reached New Delhi by train. And on the next day, they had reached Mumbai by Rajdhani Express. Pratima and Mansi had reached Mumbai Central Railway Station to pick up their boys. Then, Akash, Tejas, and Sarthak came out of the wagon and met their mothers.

"How was your trip?" Pratima asked as the boys touched her and Mansi's feet for blessings.

"It was awesome," Akash said happily. Then, they met their tour operator and said their goodbyes to them. Even Akash and Tejas said their goodbyes to Sarthak's friends. Then, they moved toward their home. After reaching home, Akash, Tejas, and Sarthak discussed with their parents all sorts of fun they had during the camp.

"So, now what's next?" Saurabh asked at the breakfast table.

"Now just going home," Pratima said.

"Why?" Saurabh asked. "Now tomorrow, Akash is going to Panchgani, Mahabaleshwar, Lonavala, and Khandala with his kaka's family. Then, he is going to Goa with his friends, and then he is making a solo trip to Rajasthan."

"Oh! Wow. His complete holidays are full of trips." Pratima was impressed.

"Why don't you send Akash and Tejas somewhere?" Saurabh asked. "See, what I believe is, this is their last longest vacation. So, let them enjoy it to the fullest. By traveling, they learn many new things."

Akash had understood what Saurabh was saying. He was right as he thought. Not everyone gets a chance to rewind the time like him. Then, after lunch, Sarthak sent all of their photos to Akash on his email address. Then, by evening, Pratima, Akash, and Tejas had left for Dhran.

The next day, Akash, Pratima, and Tejas reached Dhran. Again as Akash was late that day, he had to miss the gym. So, after breakfast, Akash and Tejas went out to play with their colony friends.

"How was your trip?" Nitya asked.

"It was really awesome," Akash replied.

"Someday we should also plan the same," Manish said.

"Yeah seriously. Traveling is the best mode of learning." Dhaval said.

"So, shall we plan a trip somewhere?" Akash asked while keeping Saurabh's words in his mind.

"Yeah, seriously we need some outings," Ankita said

"But where?" Dhaval asked.

"Anywhere. Be it Gujarat, Rajasthan, Goa, or South India." Akash said.

"Let's go to Rajasthan," Minakshi said.

"Let's ask our parents and then we will decide," Nitya said. So, during lunch, the first thing Akash asked his parents was about the trip.

"Akash, you already had a trip to the north-east. Now it's enough." Pratima said.

"Maa, please. This is my last longest holiday." Akash persuaded. But no one replied. Then, to break the silence, Prashant said while having his bite, "Through whom you all are going?"

"We will need to search online," Akash said.

"You all decide the dates and let me know. I will find a good tour operator for you." Prashant said.

"Thank you, papa," Akash said excitedly.

"Prashant please!" Pratima tried to stop Prashant.

"Pratima, just relax." Prashant said. Then he turned to Akash and said, "Akash, you are visiting so many places. Why don't you write a book on each city? Describe the city from the tourist point of view." Prashant said. So, Akash liked the idea very much.

After lunch, when Akash was in his bedroom reading his novels, he was just wondering how lucky he was. His time got rewind. He was the only one whose time had been rewind, as he thought. But one thing suddenly struck him – how did his time rewind? What price he would have to pay for this time rewind, he wondered. But still, he happily accepted it. Then, he started noting down all the detailed points regarding his summer camp. He wanted to write a book, named 'Delhi, Sikkim, Meghalaya, and Assam – from the tourist point of view.'

CHAPTER FIFTEEN

Akash was back from his Rajasthan trip. He had a wonderful trip with his friends. They visited Udaipur, Jaisalmer, Jodhpur, Chittorgarh, and Kumbhalgarh. It was their fifteen-day trip, where they visited all the forts, deserts, war memorials, zoos, national parks, and much more. As Akash was a history fan, that turned out to be his favourite trip.

The next day onwards, Akash made up his mind to be regular at the Gym. So, before going to bed, he had set the alarm for five o'clock without fail. As it was his first day at the Gym, he woke up just in time, got ready, and reached the gym by half past five.

Akash was visiting a gym for the first. He was amazed to see other people using all the equipment over there. Some were lifting heavy weights, some were doing chest exercises, and some were doing pull-ups, while some were doing exercises that he didn't know. "You are just a beginner right now. So, you just do warm-up for a couple of days." The trained said to Akash. So, he took him inside and showed him some exercise for warming up his body. While Akash was warming up, he suddenly saw Neha and Hansika over there. But, immediately some minutes after their warm-up session, they went to another room and started lifting weights. Akash guessed that they must have joined the gym on the first day of their holidays.

Akash continued the exercise he was told to do. Then after half an hour, it was time for him to leave. While leaving, he saw that Neha and Hansika too were about to leave. He knew that they would go for their lawn tennis classes. He had joined the same tennis class as them. So, he furtively moved out so that he would reach before them.

Akash had reached the tennis court on time. Over there, he saw people playing on the court while some were waiting for their chance. Then, he went to the coach and met him who was on the smaller court, teaching his younger students. He was Rahul Bhamre, who seemed to be in his forty's.

"Good morning sir," Akash said.

"Good morning, Akash," Rahul said. "Where have you been all these days?"

"Actually sir, I was out of town. I came back yesterday." Akash said.

"I thought so. Anyways, as of now, you will be taught only the basic steps. First, you master it, then I will allow you to play on the bigger court." Rahul said. "Get ready"

Akash got ready with his new racket in his hand. He was too excited about the new sport. "Remember one thing, Akash, this is not badminton. You have to hit the ball straight. You need to apply only that much force which is required." Rahul said.

"Yes sir," Akash replied. But as the coach bit him to hit the ball, he applied his full strength to hit the shot. The ball went in the air and then hit the ground outside the court.

"Oh!" Akash exclaimed. Everyone was staring at him for his shot.

"Are you playing cricket?" Rahul scolded him in front of everyone. So, Akash felt a bit awkward. "I told you to apply only that much strength which is required. Now go and get the ball." But Akash couldn't see any gate towards the place where the ball fell.

"From where I am supposed to go out?" Akash asked.

"There is only one gate. Go out from the main entrance, take your bike, and ride it throughout the road towards this side. Then, get the ball." Rahul said. Akash just stood over there wondering about the long way towards the ball. "Come on, go." Rahul said and so, Akash had to walk towards the main entrance.

While moving towards the gate, Akash saw Neha and Hansika on the main court playing tennis. He saw them hitting the shots perfectly. Then, Akash took his bicycle and started riding. He had to reach the other side of the court. But even after reaching the spot, he had to search the ball for a while. Then finally he found it. Then, while riding back, Akash wondered whether he had to go to take the ball everytime he would hit hard. He wondered what if Hansika and Neha would come to know. Then after around five minutes, he reached the ground.

Akash had a tough day on the tennis ground. For multiple times, he had go out and get the ball while hiding himself from Neha and Hansika. But no matter how much he tried to hide himself, Neha and Hansika had noticed him. Akash had realised if that continued, then he would again spoil his image in front of Neha and Hansika. Then, by around nine o'clock, he had returned.

"Akash, your S.S.C. result is out. You have scored sixty-two percent." Prashant said excitedly as Akash reached home. Prashant had checked his result online.

"Congratulations my son." Pratima hugged Akash and then kissed his forehead. "Even I had got the call from your school. They have called you all at ten o'clock."

"My son." Even Prashant hugged him with tears in his eyes. Akash knew that his percentage was too low, but still, he pretended to be happy in front of his parents. He even knew that even if it was high, it would have done no good to him. "Now go and collect your results from your school."

"Yes papa," Akash said and went to his room to get ready. Then as he was out of sigh, Pratima asked, "Prashant, is sixty-two percent enough?"

"No, it's not enough. But our son has scored more than our expectations. So, let us celebrate for a while." Prashant said.

"But he shouldn't get overconfident," Pratima warned.

"Don't worry. That won't happen." Prashant assured.

Then, Akash had his breakfast and was about to leave along with his friends. "Did you all see your results?" He asked.

"I have got only sixty-five percent," Dhaval said in dismay.

"Does sixty-five percent seem 'only' to you?" Akash asked.

"I was expecting at least seventy percent," Dhaval said.

"Dude, cheer up. I have got sixty-two percent which is less than you." Akash said. But Dhaval didn't reply and started moving. So, everyone just gave a flummoxed look at each other and started following Dhaval.

"Dhaval, as it is you are going to take admission in the science stream, you will definitely get admission with this percentage," Ankita said to encourage him.

"You have scored eighty-seven percent, so it's not going to matter to you," Dhaval said.

"Eighty-seven percent!" Akash pretended to be startled. He had known about Ankita's score for eleven years, but he had to show in front of everyone that he was shocked just like them.

Then, soon, they had reached the school. As soon as they entered the school premises, Akash was too impressed to re-create his nostalgic memories. He met his schoolmates over there after a long time and had a good talk with them. Then, they were called to their classrooms and their results were handed to them.

In the evening, when Prashant had returned home from his shop, he called Akash. "He is with his friends," Pratima said.

"Pratima, please call him. I need to talk to him." Prashant said. So Pratima went out to call Akash.

"Yes papa," Akash said as he reached.

"Now as your result is out, you go with your friends and get the admission forms from all the colleges," Prashant said. "And are you sure you want to join the arts stream for literature and History?"

"Yes, papa. I want to go for literature and history." Akash replied. "But Papa, can I go to Mumbai for my studies?"

"Akash, first you have to find out which college is good for you. We don't know any of the colleges in Mumbai." Pratima said.

"Actually, I have talked to Sarthak. He says that I can get admission over there." Akash said.

"Then you should have told me this during the daytime. I would have booked a ticket for you for tonight." Prashant said. "Anyways, pack your luggage. You and your mother leave for Mumbai by tomorrow."

"Okay, papa," Akash said. After the dinner, he had immediately packed his bag for Mumbai. He was very excited to leave for Mumbai. He knew that he would get admission over there and would get a chance to be with Hansika. Even his aim was clear, and he knew that he would be successful at a very young age. While lying on the bed, he was waiting for the day, when he would be launching his first book along with Hansika.

After two days, Akash and Pratima had reached Mumbai. As usual, they were staying at Mansi's place. Then, Akash went along with Sarthak to get all the admission forms filled. For about eight to ten colleges, they had filled out the form. But Akash was just reluctant about F. A. Iyer College where Hansika studied in his original time. He knew that she would be admitted to that college.

Then, they had reached F. A. College. It was a huge college with multiple buildings on a single campus. Over there, Akash filled out the form for B.A. while carefully selecting history and literature subjects. But over there, his eyes were continuously searching Hansika. But the crowd was so much that it wasn't possible for him to see her. So, he let it go for that day.

The next day, Akash and Pratima had reached Dhran. After reaching home, again Akash had to miss his gym and tennis classes as he was late. So, after breakfast, he went to be with his friends as usual.

"Why are you not taking admission in Dhran?" Minakshi asked while playing her shot in badminton.

"The education in Mumbai is much better than here," Akash said. He was sitting on the verandah with his other friends waiting for his chance. His friends weren't moving out of Dhran for their studies. He would miss them, but he knew what he was doing for himself. In in original time, he had done blunders, but life had given him a second chance by rewinding his time. And he didn't want to mess up again. But again while thinking of time rewinding, his mind still caught the thought of how did his time rewind. Sometimes he couldn't believe that he was in his past. He didn't know whether he should have figured it out or not.

From the next day, Akash was again regular to his gym and tennis classes. He wanted to befriend Neha and Hansika. He wanted to ask Hansika about her admission to the college. But he had to slow down or else, again he would spoil everything.

The days went on. In the morning, Akash would go to the gym and tennis classes. Then after breakfast, he would play with his friends. Then after lunch, he would do reading. Then, again in the evening, he would spend time with his friends. But still, he couldn't make Neha and Hansika his friends. Forget about making friends, he hadn't even started talking to them.

Then one fine day, Prashant called Pratima from his shop stating that he had received a call from F.A. College. Akash's admission was confirmed. His college was about to start at the end of July 2006. So, he had reached Mumbai a day prior and was staying at Mansi's place. Then, the next day he reached his college on time.

Akash was too excited about his new college life. Moreover, he was excited about being with Hansika. So, in that excitement, he reached his college before time, where he found that the gates were still closed. He waited over there and remembered his first day at his architecture college. But now, everything was fine. Then, the students started hoarding near the gate. Akash was searching for Hansika, but she couldn't be found. He was dead sure that she had been admitted to that college. She must have been late or she must be yet to get the admission, as he thought. "Hey, Akash." Akash heard a familiar voice. But as he turned around, he saw left startled.

"Shreyas!" Akash said out of shock. How come Shreyas was over there, he wondered.

"How are you?" Shreyas asked.

"I am good," Akash replied. He couldn't understand what was going on. He was already flummoxed about his time rewind, and now it was Shreyas.

"I know what are you wondering. My time has also rewind just like you." Shreyas said in a low voice.

"What!" Akash exclaimed with a bewildered look. He wondered how many people had a time rewind like him. He was not getting how that time rewind happened. Was he supposed to pay a heavy price for that, he wondered. If 'Yes' then what was the price, he didn't know.

"How did your time rewind?" Akash asked.

"I am totally blank about this, just like you?" Shreyas said.

"Hey, wait a minute. How did you come to know that I have witnessed a time rewind? And how did you come to know that I didn't have any idea about how it happened?" Akash asked.

"I don't know how I came to know. In fact, I don't know what's going on." Shreyas said. Then the gate opened and the students were let in.

While moving inside, Akash said, "Actually, I had prayed for it. So, there must be something which you must have done."

"I don't know anything buddy. Even in the future, I will be learning many new things, but I won't have any idea of its source." Shreyas. Said.

"What are you talking dude? You will be having information but you will not know from where that information came." Akash said. "Isn't it weird?"

"As if our time rewind is logical," Shreyas said. They both were in the same class. Just like their previous college, they had their seats one behind the other. Then, the class teacher came and so, everyone stood up. "Good morning children." She said. She was Mrs. Neha Punjabi. Then she took the attendance. While taking attendance, Akash was waiting for Hansika's name with full concentration. Then attendance ended, but her name wasn't announced.

Akash was shocked as well as depressed. He had wished that time rewind to be with Hansika. What was the use of it when Hansika was not with him, he thought. As much as he remembered, Hansika was from the same college. Then he guessed, she must be in the other division.

The college was over by one o'clock. After reaching home and having his lunch, Akash straight away went inside his bedroom to read his novel. He was sharing Sarthak's bedroom. The whole afternoon and evening he had spent behind his novel. Then, it was only after dinner that he took a break and joined his maasi's family to watch their favourite television show. Then by ten o'clock, he was off to bed.

The days went on. Akash had even joined a gym which was having timing from evening six o'clock to seven o'clock. By half past seven, he used to reach home. He had even found out that there was a sports ground on his college's campus. Over there, he used to practice lawn tennis and cricket.

Everyday, he used to reach college on time. But hadn't found Hansika till then. Shreyas had realized that he was in search of someone. "Hansika is not in this college." He said.

"Who is Hansika?" Akash pretended.

"She is the one whom you are searching everyday." Shreyas said.

"How do you about Hansika?" Akash asked in astonishment.

"I don't know buddy. I just know that this is not our real-time. This is just our time rewind." Shreyas said. "Maybe, there must be many people who must have faced this time rewind. And that time rewind must have placed them somewhere else."

"You mean, if Hansika is not here, that means she is too facing her time rewind. And just like we are here, she must be somewhere else." Akash said in dismay.

"Maybe your guess is right," Shreyas said. Akash had realized that Hansika wouldn't be with him. If she wasn't in that college, then Akash needed to find her. She was one of the reasons he had asked for a time rewind from God.

"But instead of focusing on Hansika, you should focus on your writing career," Shreyas suggested. So, Akash felt that he was right.

The days went on. Akash was performing well in his studies. His teachers were always calling his parents and appreciating his work. He was leading in his class and his parents were happy about that. He had even developed his sports skills and had made a good muscular body.

Akash was very happy with his new life. He had made good friendship with Sarthak's friends who had accompanied him to the summer camp and with his own classmates. He was enjoying each and every bit of his life. After every three to four months, he used to go to Lonavala – Khandala or Dhanu or Alibaug with Shreyas or Sarthak and his friends. He would take picture of each and every moment and save it. He used to note down each and every detail of those places if he happened to write a book on it from the tourist point of view.

The whole year of Akash had ended. He had completed all the novels of the Harry Potter series, noted down all the difficult words, and understood the plot. Now, he had to study for his exams. But he knew that as he had taken his favorite subjects, and so, he would be scoring the best.

"We are planning a trip to Shimla, Kullu, and Manali for twelve days after our exams. So, are you coming?" Sarthak asked Akash during the dinner.

"Let me ask at home." Akash said. So, after he had his dinner, he straight away went to his room and called Pratima.

"How is my son doing?" Prashant asked.

"Everything is good, papa." Akash said. "Actually I wanted to ask you something. Sarthak and his friends are planning a trip to Shimla, Kullu, and Manali after our exams for twelve days. So, can I go with them?"

"Sure." Prashant said. "Just let me know the fees and other details. I will transfer the amount into your account."

"Thank you, papa." Akash said.

"Take Tejas along with you. And now focus on your studies. Your exams are nearing." Prashant said.

"Yes papa. Bye." Akash said and ended the call.

Prashant was getting worried about Akash's expenses. But considering his performance in his college, he ignored. Even in the evening, when he had returned home, Pratima asked, "Did Akash talked to you about his trip?"

"Yeah. He is going to Shimla, Kullu, and Manali." Prashant said.

"Prashant, why do you allow him? Even in and around Mumbai, he is travelling a lot with his friends." Pratima said. "He had called me for this. So, I had to scold him."

"Pratima, travelling is a good source of learning. Instead I have told him to take Tejas along with him. He is doing well in his studies. In return, we can atleast let him enjoy his holidays." Prashant said.

Soon, Akash's exams were over. He had readied his luggage to go on the trip. Even Tejas had reached Mumbai on the departure's day. Then, after fifteen days trip Akash returned to Dhran.

Akash was completely changed. He had taken responsibility for many things in his house, and his parents were shocked about that. Even his colony friends were too impressed by his achievements and his muscular body. That made him feel confident. But one thing was still troubling him. How did his time actually rewind, he didn't know. How did Shreyas happened to be with him, he didn't know. Where was Hansika, he didn't know.

To find out more about Hansika, he had rejoined the same gym and tennis classes that he had joined earlier. Over there, Hansika and Neha had appeared again. But as they both didn't know him, it was risky talking to them. He had to find out where Hansika and Neha studied, but he didn't know how.

Then, his result was declared and he scored the best in the class. He was happy, but his parents were on cloud nine. For the first time, his parents felt that their son had made a good decision by taking admission in the field of his choice.

The twelfth standard days of Akash were the same. Throughout the year, he had performed well and made his parents proud. He had even finished reading his new series – 'The Lord of the Rings', noted down the difficult word, and understood the plot. Then, by the end of the year, he had already written a book with the title 'DELHI, SIKKIM, MEGHALAYA, AND ASSAM – from the tourist point of view' as he had visited those states during his summer camp a couple of years back. He had experienced new things over there. So, he had written that book from his own point of view. But, there was a challenge. He didn't know how to self-publish it. He had a bad experience of publishing his book with a publisher which didn't turn a hit. So, now he wanted to take a different option.

During his holidays, he would search online about how to self-publish a book. But he didn't get satisfactory answers. So, instead of hurrying and creating a blunder again, he preferred to wait. He had spent his whole holidays in Dhran with his friends.

"Will you have any entrance exams?" Manish asked.

"No," Akash replied.

"Wow, you are so lucky, man. I wish we too didn't have any entrance exams. We would have also got this vacation to enjoy." Dhaval said.

"Are you all continuing your studies in Dhran?" Akash said.

"I am going to Bangalore. While Manish, Dhaval, and Rohan are going to Pune. Ankita is going to Indore. And the rest are here." Dhruv said.

"By the way guys, there is good news," Akash announced. So, everyone glared at him in amazement.

"Are you serious? Which month is going on?" Rohan japed.

"You idiot, there is another news," Akash said. So, everyone had a guffaw.

"I asked that which month of the calendar is going on. I didn't say that you are expecting a baby." Rohan again jested.

"By the way Akash, what is the good news?" Minakshi asked.

"I have written a book and I am about to publish it," Akash said excitedly.

"Oh! Congratulations." Ankita said.

"What book is that?" Manish asked.

"It's regarding a tourist place from the tourist point of view," Akash said.

"Oh, that's great. We will be waiting for it." Dhruv said. Then everyone congratulated Akash for his new book. If he would publish it, he would be one of the youngest authors. But he was worried about finding a proper way to publish. But a couple of thoughts were still troubling him. How did his time rewind and why Hansika wasn't in his college, he didn't know. So, to know more about her, he joined the same gym and the tennis classes again. But over there, he couldn't gather courage to talk to Hansika and Neha.

Then, Akash's holidays had ended and his senior college had started. He had been admitted in the same college immediately after his H.S.C. result was declared. As usual, he had reached Mumbai a day prior and had reached his college before time the next day.

As Akash reached the college on the first day, he saw that Shreyas was again in his class. On seeing him, he would always ask himself how the time rewind for him and Shreyas. And why Hansika was not in his college. But, somehow he had accepted his fate and had decided to move on. He had prepared himself mentally to avoid the thought of Hansika.

He had reached his class and had sat at his desk. As usual, Shreyas was behind him. All the students also started entering the class. There was a bit of silence in class as most of the students were new. Then, the class teacher arrived. She was Mrs. Shruti Iyer. She introduced her subject and started taking attendance. But there was a surprise for Akash. As Mrs. Iyer was taking attendance, he heard her calling 'Hansika Galani'. Akash turned around and saw Hansika replying 'Yes ma'am'. Oh! Hansika was here. Akash got excited about seeing her in the class. But she was at the far end. So, he decided to sit with her the next day.

The next day had arrived. So, Akash had reached the college much earlier than usual. After entering the class, he sat on the bench behind Hansika. Then, he saw Hansika entering the class and taking her seat in front of him. Hansika and Akash saw each other. She had realized that Akash too was from Dhran, as she would see him in the gym and at tennis classes. Then, a boy arrived who said to Akash, "Hey, it's my bench."

"I have already arranged my stuff over here. Can you please shift somewhere else?" Akash requested. Hansika noticed them.

"But I was sitting over here yesterday." The boy said.

"What's going on?" The class teacher asked as she arrived.

"Ma'am this is my place, and this boy has occupied it." The boy complained.

"Why are you being so childish? Is your name written on it? Go and sit somewhere else." The class teacher said. So, the boy went to some other desk. Akash saw that Shreyas was staring at him in amazement. Then, the class began.

During the lunch break, when Akash and Shreyas were moving towards the canteen, Shreyas said, "Did you talk to her?"

"Not yet," Akash replied.

"Then what was the use of fighting with that boy over the desk?" Shreyas asked. Then, they saw Hansika in the canteen. She was alone and ordering her dishes. "Go," Shreyas said to Akash. So he furtively reached the canteen and ordered some sandwiches while standing next to Hansika.

"Hi," Akash said.

"Hello," Hansika said with a smile.

"I guess you are from Dhran," Akash said.

"Yeah. We were in the same gym and tennis classes." Hansika said. Then, she took her tray and started moving. Then, Akash's tray was also ready. So, he took it and moved towards Hansika's table.

"Can we join you?" Akash asked politely.

"Yeah, sure." Hansika said. So, Akash and Shreyas had their seats and accompanied her. They had a good time chatting with each other. Then, they paid their bills and moved towards their class.

Akash liked Hansika very much. He was finding a way to talk to her. He would ask some stationery things, pretending that he didn't have it. And so, Hansika happily lends him those things. He would have a proper watch on her, watching what she was doing or where she was stuck. He would always try to help her out and she would like it. And so, their friendship began.

Akash's performance was getting better day by day. Even he had started writing his next book – Rajasthan: from the tourist point of view. When he had visited Rajasthan along with his childhood friends, he had noted down all the required points. He would even write amazing articles on any topic during any college event. He had made a good impression in front of everyone. So, he finally had a good friend's circle of Akshat, Akansha, Pankaj, Pranjal, Monish, Ashutosh, Shreyas and Hansika.

But there was a twist. Akash's new friends had a habit of smoking and drinking. So, Akash was a bit uncomfortable with them. They would always ask Akash to try a shot or have a cigarette. But he would always avoid it, as he was aware of his background.

"Akash, I know you aren't comfortable with them. But think of Hansika. You have to be with them to be with her. Even you need to be socializing for your book's success." Shreyas persuaded him during their break.

"Hey, how do you know about my book?" Akash was astonished. "Yeah, I remember, you don't know."

Once, during their lunch break, Hansika asked Akash, "Where do you stay in Dhran?"

"Near Sardar Patel Chowk." Akash replied. "And you?"

"I stay in Jay Nagar," Hansika replied.

Akash had made a good connection with Hansika. They would often travel on some weekends to Lonavala, Khandala, Dhanu, or any nearby amazing places. But again there was something which Akash hadn't expected.

Once, they both were on a ride to Lonavala. But over there, Akash found something about Hansika that he wasn't aware about. While still on the bike, Hansika took out a packet of cigarettes and started smoking one. Akash was startled to see that. "You smoke?" Akash asked in astonishment.

"Yes," Hansika replied. "Do you have any problem?"

"It's not good," Akash said. But suddenly Hansika interjected, "Akash, now please don't start."

"Hansika, it causes cancer." Akash tried to convince her.

"Aye hello. I know all this." Hansika warned. "I even drink. But I have been trying to quit it since last year. Even my parents have tried to stop me. But it's not happening. And if you have any problem, then you may leave."

"Okay, just chill," Akash said to calm her down. He didn't want to hurt her, though he didn't like her smoking. His parents would never allow a girl to be their daughter-in-law who smoked. But still, he accepted her.

"By the way, there is good news I want to give you," Hansika said.

"What good news?" Akash asked.

"I am writing a book. And after two months, I am going to publish it." Hansika said.

"Oh! Wow. Congratulations." Akash said. "How are you going to publish it?"

"I am going to self-publish it on Amazon Kindle," Hansika said. "Actually I have joined an academy for writing and publishing. Its name is – Vibgyor Academy for Authors. It's owned and run by Author Shruti Kore at Carter Road, Bandra."

"I too want to join. What's the fee?" Akash asked.

"Eleven thousand rupees for one year," Hansika said. "If you want, you can join from this coming January."

"Okay. I will talk to my parents and let you know." Akash said. Then they moved on.

Akash was so deeply engrossed in being with Hansika that he wasn't aware of anything right or wrong. He loved a lot being with her. Throughout their journey, he was just thinking about when and how to propose her. Then, by nine o'clock at night, he had reached home after dropping Hansika at her place. But as soon as he reached home, Mansi and Sarthak were staring at him in amazement.

"What happened?" Akash asked.

"How was it?" Mansi asked.

"What?" Akash asked. "The trip was good."

"I am not asking about the trip. I am asking about your experience with your girlfriend." Mansi said in a playful way.

"Girlfriend!" Akash was startled. "But I was out with my friends."

"Oh my dear, don't be under the impression that I don't come to know anything." Mansi said while playfully pinching his cheek. "Your phone was unreachable. So, I had called Sarthak to talk to you. But he told me that you were with Hansika."

"Did you want me to get something for you?" Akash asked with the hint of blush on his face. He wanted to change the topic.

"Sarthak, look at the blush on his face." Mansi said to Sarthak and so they all started laughing. "I wanted to ask you till when you will be returning."

"Dude, you are too ahead." Sarthak teased him.

"Actually she is not my girlfriend yet. But someday she will be." Akash said with more blush.

"Okay, now get fresh and come. The food is ready." Mansi said. So, Akash furtively got ready and came for the dinner. Then, after the dinner, he straight away went to Sarthak's bedroom and called Pratima.

"How is my son going?" Pratima asked.

"I am good maa," Akash said. "You say."

"I am good too," Pratima said.

"Actually maa, there is a class for authors at Carter Road. Can I join it from January?" Akash asked.

"But have you inquired everything about it?" Pratima asked.

"No, this Saturday I will go." Akash replied.

"Talk to your father about this," Pratima said and passed the phone to Prashant.

"Yes beta, how are you?" Prashant asked.

"I am good papa," Akash said. "Actually papa, there is an academy for authors at Carter Road. I want to join it. Its fee is eleven thousand rupees for one year."

"First find out the details. I will transfer the amount to your account. Then, go for it," Prashant said.

"Thank you, papa," Akash said happily.

Akash had received a call form Dhaval after some days. They were planning a party on the thirty first of December in Dhran. But Akash didn't give any confirmation as he wanted to spend the New Year's Eve with Hansika. He just pretended to have plans with his Mumbai friends, even though he didn't know what his college friends would plan. Then, on thirty first of December, his college friends had planned to visit a nightclub for the New Year party. Over there, they enjoyed to the fullest. But when his friends including Shreyas were having alcoholic drinks, Akash would just stay back. He would just stare at Hansika in amazement while she gulped her shots. His friends would bit him to try, but he would refrain.

Then, January had arrived. Akash had completed all the formalities for admission to the author's academy. From the first day, Akash had joined the classes along with Hansika. He was very happy and excited about the class as he would get knowledge about writing and publishing as well and he would be with Hansika over here too.

"How does Beer, vodka, tequila, and everything you have taste like?" Akash asked Hansika once when they were having some free time during their classes.

"Dude, you stay away from it. You are just a kid." Hansika japed.

"No, I am not a kid." Akash said.

"Now don't tell me that you want to try. It's not for you, buddy." Hansika said. But Akash was confused. He wanted to try those drinks to be like Hansika, but even he didn't want to cheat his parents. He didn't know what to decide.

Akash and Hansika would attend their college and author's academy everyday without fail. As they both had a passion for writing, they both were doing well at both places. After knowing Akash's performance, even Pratima and Prashant were happy. They would happily talk to him about his subjects and he would happily explain everything. The way he showed his excitement showed how confident and eager he was.

Then, February had arrived. Akash had made sure that he would propose to Hansika on Valentine' day. He wanted to propose to her for a long, but couldn't gather the courage for that. But now, as she was his good friend, he was confident about her accepting his proposal.

It was the fourteenth of February. Akash wanted to surprise her. He wanted to call Hansika somewhere, which was a beautiful place. So, he chose marine lines. Akash had told Shreyas and all his friends about her and so, they had helped him in making all the arrangements for decoration and cake cutting. Then, Akash made a call to Hansika.

"Hi Hansika. Guess what, there is a surprise for all of us." Akash said excitedly.

"What surprise?" Hansika asked eagerly.

"Actually Shreyas has brought his girlfriend to meet us." Akash said. So, Shreyas gave a baffled look at him, wondering about what he was saying.

"Is it?" Hansika asked. "But where?"

"At Marine lines. We are waiting for you." Akash said.

"I will be there in thirty minutes." Hansika excitedly replied. Then, as Akash cut the call, he saw Shreyas glaring at him while his other friends were having a guffaw.

"Dude, actually I wanted to make her eager to reach here. But I couldn't tell her that I wanted to propose her." Akash explained. Then, within half an hour, Hansika was there.

"Where is the new comer of our group?" Hansika asked Shreyas. But no one replied.

Akash had got tensed on seeing Hansika. He was going to propose her. Then, he gathered confidence within himself, held Hansika's hand, and brought her in the center. Hansika wondered what was going on. Then, Akash removed the diamond ring from his pocket, bend on his knees, and said, "Hansika, I love you."

Hansika was startled. She wasn't sure about what reply she would give. She didn't want to hurt Akash. But she even didn't want to accept. "Akash, I guess I am not ready yet for this." She said.

"It's okay. You can take your time." Akash said.

"It's not regarding time. It's regarding you." Hansika said. "Our thinking and background doesn't match. I don't think so, we can be a good pair."

"Oooo." Everyone teased Akash. He was hurt. He hadn't expected that reply from her. She was one of the reasons why Akash wanted a time rewind. But it was just a waste. But still, Akash accepted her reply halfhearted and stood up.

"Akash, you can do one thing. If you have this Champaign, then Hansika will be yours." Pranjal said while removing the Champaign form her bag. They had brought the bottles for the celebration.

"Yooo." Everyone screamed to tease Akash.

"No ways, guys." Akash said.

"Yes." Hansika said in a romantic way. Everyone fell silent. "If you have this, you have me." Akash felt numb. He was flummoxed. He was getting another chance to get Hansika. But his parents wouldn't accept him as a drunkard. But who would tell his parents, he wondered. So he stared in Hansika's eyes and accepted the challenge.

"Yooo." Everyone started screaming loudly for Akash. Then, Akash uncorked the bottle, pouter the Champaign into the glass, and started drinking. But as soon as he had the first couple of gulps, he started feeling sick. He wanted to vomit.

"Yuck." Akash said while making a weird face. He didn't like the taste. "What shit is this?"

"Dude. Welcome to the club." Ashutosh said while patting his back. They even took his pictures.

"But you have to finish it." Akansha said to encourage him. So, Akash stared at the glass and then to Hansika who was again staring at him. Then, he gulped the full glass.

Akash was feeling sicker. So, immediately went to the parapet wall and started vomiting in the sea. Shreyas brought a bottle of water for him. "Take it easy." He said. Akash had some water and then, he was okay. Then,

Hansika walked towards him while he was wiping his face. He wondered now what she would say. "Yes." She said.

CHAPTER SEVENTEEN

Finally, Akash and Hansika were together. Every day, they would go to college and their academy together and spend time over there. They would even sometimes go for dinner and movies. But that was eventually increasing Akash's expenses. Every month, Prashant would provide him with pocket money, but that always proved insufficient. So Akash had to ask for money again.

Akash had started drinking and smoking just like Hansika and his college friends. His friends would even take pictures and post them on their social media pages. But he couldn't as he didn't want anyone related to his family to see his pictures in which he was drinking or smoking. Even before going back to his maasi's place, he would make sure that his mouth wasn't stinking.

Then, Akash's final exams had ended. And immediately after some days, the happiest moment of his life was about to happen. His both the books were about to launch at the academy's conclave. He immediately called Pratima and heralded her about the news.

"Oh, is it?" Pratima asked. She was too excited. "Congratulations my son. I am so happy for you."

"What happened?" Prashant asked as he heard the conversation.

"Akash's books are getting launched at the Vibgyor authors' conclave on the fifteenth of April." Pratima said while passing the phone to him.

"Oh, congratulations son." Prashant said.

"Thank you, papa. You, maa, and Tejas have to come." Akash said.

"Yes, of-course." Prashant said.

Then, the conclave day had arrived. Pratima, Prashant, and Tejas had reached Mumbai the same morning. They had reached Mansi's place on time. "Hey, how are you?" Mansi hugged Pratima as they entered. "Congratulations for your son."

"Thank you didi." Pratima said. Then, Akash came out and took his parents' blessings.

"How are you maa, papa?" Akash asked.

"We are good." Prashant said. "Is your preparation for the conclave done?"

"Yes papa, everything is done." Akash said.

"Now you all get fresh and have your breakfast. Then we will leave." Mansi said. So, they got ready and had their breakfast. Then, they had left.

Akash and his family had reached the conclave's venue on time. Even Hansika and her parents had reached over there. Akash and Hansika introduced their parents to each other. They all had a good time over there.

Akash's and Hansika's books were launched. The launch happened in the best way in front of all the media persons and personalities. Akash and Hansika had a wider platform for their books. And so, from that moment onwards, they had started receiving orders for their books. Akash saw that Prashant and Pratima were having the happiest day of their life. They were so happy that they weren't able to control their emotions. Seeing his parents happy, Akash wondered if he could have made them happy in his original time.

The next day, Akash and Hansika reached Dhran along with their families. Akash immediately got ready, had his breakfast, and went out. His parents thought that he must have gone to meet his colony friends. But after sometime, all his colony friends came to meet him.

"I thought he must have been with you people." Pratima said.

"No aunty, he is not with us." Dhaval said. "Anyways, we will meet after he returns." He added and left.

After sometime, when all of Akash's friends were busy in playing, they suddenly saw Akash reaching over there along with Hansika.

"Hey everyone." Akash said as he halted over there.

"Hey, hi." Ankita said. Everyone was astonished to see a new girl along with Akash.

"By the way guys, she is Hansika." Akash said. So, everyone just gave a baffled look at him. They had guessed that she was his girlfriend. "Yes, you all are thinking right."

"Oh!" Ankita said. Then, she looked at Hansika and said, "Hi, I am Ankita and this is Dhaval, Minakshi, Dhruv, Nitya, Tejas, Rohan, Manish, and Sejal. And welcome to the group."

"Thank you." Hansika said happily.

"Guys, can we go for lunch?" Akash asked.

"Of-course. You are bringing Hansika here for the first time. We should have a treat from you." Dhaval japed.

"Yes of-course you should have a treat. But for now you will have to pay on behalf of me." Akash japed back.

Then, everyone went for the lunch. Akash introduced everyone to Hansika. Everyone was in a playful mood and even did some mischief with her, but she didn't seem to like that. Even she was expecting some non-vegetarian dishes along with some drinks. But it was a pure vegetarian meal.

She even nudged Akash and hinted him about what she wanted.

"No." Akash muttered. So, Hansika glowered at him

"What happened?" Dhruv asked as he saw both of them in a cold fight.

"It's nothing. She is just asking if we could have non-veg. so, I said 'No'." Akash said. Everyone was startled to hear that. They never had someone in their group having non-veg. But Hansika felt abashed.

After the lunch, everyone was moving towards their home. "Akash, does your parents know that they are having a daughter in-law?" Ankita asked. But Hansika was startled to hear that. She wasn't expecting to marry Akash. But over there, his friends were visualizing things far beyond their imagination.

"No. they don't know her." Akash said. "And guys, please don't let them know."

"But Tejas already knows." Rohan said.

"Don't worry. I won't tell anyone." Tejas said.

Then they had reached Sardar Patel Chowk. "Guys, you all continue. I will drop Hansika and return." So, everyone agreed and moved towards their home.

"Such cheap friends you are having." Hansika taunted while they were on their way.

"What's wrong?" Akash asked as he was baffled. He was expecting Hansika to enjoy his friends' company. But the thing seemed opposite.

"They don't drink, they don't have non-veg, and they are bothered about our marriage." Hansika said.

"Aye, they are unaware about me drinking and smoking." Akash warned. "Don't let them know."

"Huh! Forget about telling them, I won't even like to meet them again." Hansika said. "Bloody losers."

"What's the problem?" Akash asked.

"Why are you so afraid about your parents and friends for knowing about our relation and your drinking habits? If you can hide these things from them then you must be hiding something from me too, isn't it." Hansika said.

"Hey, it's nothing like that." Akash said.

"Who the hell gave them the right for talking about my marriage?" Hansika asked.

"It's okay. Why are you getting so hyper? As it is someday we are getting married." Akash said.

"Aye hello, who told you that I am going to marry you? Are your parents going to allow me to smoke, drink, or have non-veg at your home?" Hansika asked. But Akash fell numb after hearing her. He was under the impression that Hansika will be his forever. But he was wrong. His parents were too simple who needed a daughter in-law like Neha. Then without a word, they both rode on.

Akash had dropped Hansika at her place. "You are like this because of these losers. I was so excited for this lunch, but you people spoiled everything." Hansika said. "That's why I hadn't accepted your proposal in the beginning. Because I knew you. I was a fool who thought that if you can drink and smoke, then we can be together. I was really a fool who accepted you that day. Now don't try to make me meet these people." She added and went inside.

Akash was deeply hurt that day. His childhood friends were the best part of his life. He didn't like those words about them from Hansika's mouth. But it was he, who had wished for a time rewind so that he could be with her. But while he was on his way towards his home, his destiny had arranged one more surprise for him.

As Akash reached home, he saw that Prashant's scooter was parked outside his house. He wondered why Prashant was home at that time. He went inside and saw Pratima, Prashant, and Tejas waiting for him. Three of them were staring at him and so, he felt a bit droll. "Is everything fine?" He asked.

"Come here." Prashant said. Then, he showed him the cigarette box. "What's this?"

Akash had realized that he was caught. "I.....don't know." He hesitated to talk.

"Your mother found this in your bag." Prashant said. Pratima was staring at him. But he couldn't reply. So, realizing the fact, Prashant gave a tight slap on his face. Akash help his cheek while looking down in chagrin. "Is this for we are sending you to college?"

Akash eyes were welled with unfallen tears. "Do you have any idea of what I have to go through to manage your expenses? And you are having all this." Prashant asked, but Akash just gave a numb reply.

"Since when are you smoking?" Pratima asked.

"Since past couple of months." Akash said. His head was still down.

"And what made you start having this?" Prashant asked. "You are doing well with your books, you are scoring well in your exams, you have a good friends, you are enjoying each and every second. I haven't said 'no' to any of your demands even when I couldn't afford it. And this is what you are giving us in return." Prashant threw the cigarette box on his face.

"I want to talk to that girl whom you had taken for lunch. She is your classmate, isn't she?" Pratima said.

"But maa, she isn't aware about all this." Akash lied as he knew that Hansika would get more irritated if Pratima talked to her about his habits. Then, Akash took a deep breath and said, "I am sorry maa."

"We don't want your sorry. We want your commitment that you won't be smoking henceforth." Prashant said. Tejas was just looking on. Even he was shocked to know about his brother. Then, Prashant took a deep breath and added, "Son, we care for you. We love you. This poison is not going to do anything good to you. Akash, promise me that you will give up smoking." Prashant held Akash's hands in his hands.

"Yes papa, I promise that I won't have this again." Akash said. So, Prashant hugged him and kissed him on his forehead.

It was night. Before going to bed, Pratima asked Prashant, "Will our son stop smoking?"

"We will have to watch him. But don't worry, he will give up his bad habits." Prashant said. He was worried for his son. He knew that his son wouldn't stop so easily. But still he had to find some way.

The years went on. Akash had become successful author since his college days. He would publish two-to-three novels every year. Every year, he would bring his parents to the book launch conclave and launch his novel. Prashant and Pratima were too happy on seeing their son achieve success at such a young age.

By Akash's last year in his college, social media was widely spread. He and his parents would get appreciation from all their known ones. Even the ones, who were not in touch for years had started calling his parents and appreciating his work. Akash was the first one from his family and friends who had started earning since his college days.

Akash had moved far ahead in his life. He had become so successful that most of the publishers were after him to publish his book. He had even managed to buy a flat for himself and his family in Navi Mumbai. But it was only he who had shifted over there. Prashant and Pratima wanted to stay in Dhran till their both the children were settled and married. Even Hansika was far behind him. She was jealous of him. So, she had a plan to match with him.

"I am ready to marry you." Hansika said to Akash once when they were on a date. Akash was happy for Hansika's decision. Finally he had succeeded in convincing Hansika. But, at the same time, he was nervous. He didn't know whether his parents would accept Hansika or not.

Akash had a work to do before his marriage. He wanted to publish his dream novel which he had written in his original time. It was his dream to make the story a super hit, which would be read my millions and would have a movie on it.

Akash had become a successful author by then. He had unintentionally completely left his old childhood friends with no contacts. He would go to parties, out-stations, or anywhere only with his new friends. His old friends would always try to contact him through Tejas. But he would always find some reasons to end the chat. Even his parents would always make him understand the importance of old friends. But he had become so arrogant that he would just have arguments with them. Most of the times, he would return home completely drunk. So, Prashant and Pratima would always warn him on call to give up those addiction.

"Maa, papa, I know what I am doing. I am not the only one who is having all this. And it's completely fine." Akash argued.

"Akash, we are your parents. We know what is good for you and what is not." Prashant said.

"I know that you both are my parents. But I even know that I am your son and I can handle myself." Akash said.

Pratima and Prashant had realized that they were losing their son. They would even see his objectionable pictures on his social media pages and that would disturb them a lot.

Akash had again made himself busy for his new novel. He had the story inside his mind. So, he again started typing it in his computer. And soon, after a couple of months, his story was finished. He had already pre-marketed it and had received thousands of orders even before the launch of his book. He had started earning before the publishing, and that wasn't a big deal for him. But still he wasn't satisfied with that. He wanted a bid slice. And for that, he wanted to arrange a great launch. So, before making a decision he had made a call to his parents.

"Maa, my new book is complete and soon I want launch it and publish it." Akash said.

"That's really good, my child. I know my boy has grown up now. We are confident about you and your book. It will definitely succeed." Pratima said. "Talk to your father about this."

"Hi beta, tell me how's your writing work going on?" Prashant seemed a bit tired. He was afraid of losing his son, and that could be felt through his voice.

"Papa, I am planning to launch my new book at Hotel Taaj. I want to have a grand launch for it." Akash said.

"That's really great. When are you planning to do that?" Prashant asked.

"Within this month." Akash said. "I have just informed you and maa. I still need to talk to the hotel."

"Okay. All the best." Prashant said.

Soon, the day had arrived when Akash's dream book was to be launched. He was launching the book by himself. His parents had reached Mumbai a day earlier and were too excited for the son's book launch. He would look at his book again and again but still feel as if the book was new to him. Whenever he held his book in front of his eyes, his satisfaction was wordless. Finally, his book for which he had wished the time rewind was going to be launched.

Akash, Hansika and his parents had reached the venue before time. Even his new and old friends had visited on time. Akash had made sure about all the arrangements. He had even invited his mentor author Shruti Kore. Then, he introduced her to his parents. "Your son is one of my vibrant students. He has achieved a lot at a very young age." Shruti Kore said.

"Thank you ma'am. It's just because of you he is here. That's it." Prashant said. He and Pratima were too happy for their son's praise. Then, the guests started arriving and the function started. But during the function, Akash was just bothered about his new friends and was completely ignorant to his old childhood friends. They had felt offended but they didn't utter a word.

Akash's book was launched at a very grand level. It was his dream come true. All the media persons had noted his achievements and had started publishing. From that day onwards, Akash had started receiving good number of orders for his book on his website. Even international publishers had started calling him. They were ready to publish his new book on a wider level and were ready to pay him as per his choice.

Akash had become a successful author. Everywhere, there was only his name on the readers' lips. Then, one of the Bollywood producers had also approached him. He wanted to make a movie on his novel's story. So, Akash agreed and signed the contract.

Akash had made a huge bungalow in Dhran. And then, the biggest day of his life had arrived. He was getting married to Hansika. On his wedding day, he happened to see Neha accompanying Hansika. On seeing Neha, he suddenly remembered how his time actually rewind. What was the cost he would have to pay for it, he didn't know. But still, his biggest dream had come true. He was a successful author, his dream book was a success, and he was getting married to Hansika.

CHAPTER EIGHTEEN

Akash and Hansika were happily married. Immediately on the next day, they both had left for the honeymoon to Europe for fifteen days. Over there, they spend their beautiful days very well. They would visit all the bars, casinos, and all the tourist places over there. But by mistake, Hansika had forwarded the pictures in their family WhatsApp group. So, on seeing Akash and Hansika having alcohol, Pratima and Prashant had got offended. They even had an argument on the online video call over the topic.

"Akash, we aren't staying with your parents anymore." Hansika warned after the video call. "This is my life, Akash. Forget about your parents, I haven't given any rights even to my parents to decide anything for me."

"Hansika, its okay. Even I have a fight with them to support you. But that doesn't mean that we should leave them." Akash tried to persuade her.

"And you think that your fight with your parents is going to make everything right, isn't it?" Hansika taunted. "Do you know what the problem with you guys is? You all just want to be stuck with your stagnant old thinking. I don't know how I am going to manage with those oldies."

"Hansika, they are my parents. Mind your words." Akash raised his voice.

"Huh!" Hansika snapped and went out of the room. While Akash just stood over there wondering how his parents would manage with Hansika. Then, after two week, they were back to Dhran

Akash and Hansika had preferred to stay in Dhran at their new bungalow. But, again there seemed a twist. Hansika was least interested in doing the house chores. In the beginning, Pratima wouldn't disturb them in the morning as they were a new couple. But during the day, she would just prefer to do only the easy tasks at home and spend her time watching online movies and on social media. While Akash would be in his studio working on his new book, he would think that even Hansika was working on her novel. But he was wrong.

Once Pratima paid a surprise visit to Akash's studio. "Oh, maa!" Akash was shocked to see her over there. She seemed a bit disturbed. "Do you need something?"

"I need to talk to you" Pratima said while having a seat. "Akash, since days I am observing that Hansika is not at all interested in doing any kind of work. And whenever I try to explain her, she reacts like as if it's only she who is doing all the work and not me. I don't know how to make her understand."

"Maa, she must be with her writing work." Akash said. He knew that nothing could be done regarding Hansika's behavior.

"What writing work? I don't see her doing any writing work." Pratima said. "I am not complaining about her as I don't want to create a rift between you both. But you have to make her understand about her duties." Pratima gave a pause expecting Akash to take some action. "I must leave." She added and went upstairs. Akash wondered about Pratima's words. He was under the impression that Hansika was working on her book. So, to enquire about the truth, he decided to give surprise visit not once but multiple times at home in the gap of every two-to-three days. And over there, he would always find that Hansika would be in her bedroom spending time on her mobile or just lying on the sofa watching television or just doing nothing. Rarely did he find her in the kitchen or with her writing stuff.

One fine day, Akash went upstairs surprisingly as usual and again found out Hansika in the balcony chatting with her mother. She saw Akash standing behind her and so, she ended the call. "What happened?" She asked in astonishment.

"What's the update regarding your book?" Akash asked.

"I am still writing it." Hansika said.

"But whenever I come here, you are doing nothing regarding your book. Even you are not helping maa in the household work." Akash said.

"What do you know about what I am doing and not doing?" Hansika's mood was on the verge of boil.

"I am just saying what I am seeing." Akash warned and left before they would have a big fight. He had started missing Neha a lot. She was never like Hansika. Even though she didn't like him, she had a good respect for Pratima and Prashant. She would always accompany Pratima in her household work without fail, no matter what the situation was. He was struggling to make his career when Neha was with him. But still Neha used to support him and his family. But the case of Hansika was totally opposite. Akash had realized that the price for his time rewind was the peace, love, and bonding of his family.

Once, Neha had happened to visit Akash and Hansika along with her husband. She and her husband had a good time with Akash's family. When they were chatting, Akash realized that Neha, Pratima, and Prashant were having the same kind of laughter and joy which they used to have in

Akash's original time. He had realized that Neha was the prefect daughter-in-law for his parents.

Then, Neha saw that it was only Pratima who was bringing all the snacks and tea from the kitchen. Hansika was just busy chattering with her. So, she immediately went to the kitchen to help Pratima.

"Hey wait, where are you going?" Hansika tried to stop her.

"Aunty is doing everything. Let me help her." Neha said as she reached the kitchen.

"Aye, it's okay child. You go and sit." Pratima said as Neha was trying to grab the tray from her hand.

"Aunty, it's okay. I am like you daughter and not a guest." Neha said as she took the tray. On seeing Neha helping her mother-in-law, even Hansika went to the kitchen to help Pratima. Pratima was overwhelmed on seeing Neha's actions. She wished if Neha was her daughter-in-law. Akash was seeing everything and had realized what he had lost for his time rewind. But again the same question arose – how did his time rewind. It had been years but still he hadn't found the answer. He had only figured out what price he had to pay, and he was paying it.

The days went on. Akash's new book was about to release. It was the second part of his previous book. He was planning to self-publish it. For that he had organized a grand launch again at Hotel Taaj.

Akash was on a position where he could launch his own book without any external help. He had arranged everything over there in the best way possible. Arrangement for media and celebrities were also done right. Then, Akash saw his childhood friends arrive. So, immediately he went to them to meet them. "Hey, how's everyone?" He asked while hugging everyone.

"We are good. Congratulation for your new book." Dhaval said halfheartedly. Then Akash saw his new friends arrive. "Guys, you all carry on. I will be there in a minute." He said and went to meet his new friends. Dhaval, Dhruv, Ankita, Minakshi, Sejal, Rohan, Nitya, and Manish were too eager to meet Akash. But they just saw him having a good talk with his new friends. They again felt offended. "Guys, it's useless to be here. He has moved far ahead." Ankita said.

"Yeah, even Hansika is not bothered about meeting us. Just look at her. She is comfortable with Akash's new friends but not with us." Dhaval said.

"But this is not fair, guys. We have come here just to meet him and he is ignoring us. If he had to do this then why did he invite us? Even in Dhran, he doesn't have time to meet us." Manish said.

"Guys, let's move." Rohan said and so, they had started moving out.

"Hey everyone." Everyone stopped and saw Tejas calling them. "How are you all?"

"We are good. You say." Manish said while hugging him.

"Come inside. Maa and papa were asking about you all." Tejas said. They all gave a baffled look at each other, wondering whether to move out or stay.

"Let's move inside." Dhaval said, just for the sake Pratima and Prashant. So, they all moved in.

The conclave was too huge which took their whole day. Then, Akash's book was launched which turned. In his speech, Akash praised everyone including his parents, Hansika, his in-laws, and even his new friends. But he didn't have even a single word for his childhood friends. They were too hurt and so, they left the conclave without informing Akash.

For his new book's launch, Akash had arranged a grand party the next day for all his friends. But for that, he had completed neglected his childhood friends. After the party was done, Akash and Hansika had returned home in a complete drunkard state. Their eyes were dark red and they both were struggling to stand properly. As they both entered their home, they saw Pratima and Prashant standing right in front of them.

"You both are still awake!" Akash exclaimed as he was shocked.

"We had to be awake. We were worried as we knew in what state you both would return." Prashant taunted.

"Papa, can we discuss about all this in the morning?" Hansika asked while trying to move inside.

"Bhabi, bhaiya, what's wrong with you both?" Tejas asked as he too was startled to see their condition.

"Aye, it's none of your business." Akash warned Tejas.

"Let it be Tejas." Prashant said and moved inside followed by Pratima. Even Tejas went inside after cursing Akash and Hansika.

Next morning, the first thing Akash did was to make a video call to his childhood friends. But none received the call even after multiple attempts. Akash had realized something was wrong. So to clear his doubt, he made an audio call to Dhaval.

"Hello." Dhaval said formally.

"Hey. Why did you people left to early from the conclave?" Akash asked.

"We were getting late for the bus." Dhaval said.

"Okay." Akash said. But Dhaval didn't seem liking to continue the talk. So, to break the silence, Akash asked, "What's wrong?"

"It seems you have moved far ahead of us." Dhaval taunted.

"No buddy, I haven't moved anywhere. I am still with you guys." Akash tried to clear.

"Is it? But we didn't find you with us in your conclave." Dhaval said. "Anyways, we will talk later." He added and ended the call. Akash had realized what Dhaval meant. He had lost his childhood friends. His childhood friends were the reason behind his writing career. They were the first one for whom he had written his first poem. How could he forget them, he didn't realise. He had started realizing the price for his time rewind.

After somedays, when Akash and Hansika were in Dhran, Hansika had come to know that she was pregnant. First, she excitedly gave the good news to Akash. "Akash, guess what! I am pregnant."

"What!" Akash got excited. But, he suddenly remembered the moment when Neha had given him the good news for the first time. His son Baadal was about to be born. He stood there, as if petrified, while wondering about Baadal. His childhood memories were suddenly got played inside his mind. He remembered the first time when he held Baadal in his hands, the days when he used to play with him, how he would be awakened the whole night and make Baadal sleep, his first birthday, and everything else. His eyes were welled with tears. But Baadal was not with him and he had to accept it.

"Akash!" Hansika called. "What happened?" Akash got awakened from his day dreaming. "Nothing. Let's give this good news to maa and papa."

Akash and Hansika had reached down. Prashant and Pratima were already there on the dining table having breakfast. They both looked at Hansika and Akash but didn't give any reaction, as if they were tired of them. "Maa, papa, there is a good news. I am expecting a baby."

"Oho!" Prashant said in excitement. Even Pratima got happy hearing the news.

"But right now, first we should go and consult the gynecologist." Pratima said. So, they agreed and went to the gynecologist at eleven o'clock. Pratima had taken the appointment on the phone call. The doctor inspected Hansika and confirmed her pregnancy. She was second month pregnant.

After returning home, Hansika immediately called her parents and gave the good news. They were extremely happy for her. They too warned her about not to spread the news too early, and so she agreed. Then after that, she went to her bedroom and secretly called her best friends Neha and heralded her about her pregnancy.

"Oh wow! Even I have a good news." Neha said excitedly. "Even I am expecting a baby. Mine too is second month going on."

"Oh! Is it? Congratulations to both of us." Hansika said.

"Same to you sweetheart. But for now, don't give this news to people outside your family. Not even to our friends. Even I haven't informed anyone." Neha said.

"Oh! Okay." Hansika said.

"Now I need to go. We will talk on this later." Neha said and ended the call.

Hansika was already avoiding works, be it her writing work or household work. And now, she had got much bigger reason to just lie down the whole day. In the beginning, she would just order Pratima and Akash for everything. Then, when the things went too far, Pratima said, "Hansika, you need to move your body to keep yourself fit. It will affect your baby."

"Maa, I know what I am doing." Hansika said.

"No, you don't. That's why I need to guide you. Now get up. Move your muscles so that it will help you during your delivery." Pratima said while helping her get up.

The days went on. Hansika's situation was worsening day by day. But unlike last time, Akash would take care of her properly. He would regularly take her to the gynecologist, bring fruits and medicines for her, accompany her on a walk, talk to the baby, and much more. Whenever he would see Hansika, he would remember Neha. But the thought that Neha and Baadal wouldn't be with him was not getting inside his mind.

But the worst part during Hansika's pregnancy was, she wouldn't give up cigarettes and alcoholic drinks. Whenever she and Akash would return from a night-out party, they would always have an argument with Pratima and Prashant.

"Why don't you both understand that drinking and smoking is not good for your baby? Atleast for the child's sake give up that for sometime." Prashant warned.

"Papa, it's not like that I haven't tried giving up drinking. But it's not happening. What am I supposed to do? Even I have consulted the gynecologist. But it's not working. And there are many pregnant women who smoke and drink." Hansika seemed to be of tough hide. Prashant and Pratima had realized that it was useless explaining Akash and Hansika.

In the seventh month, Hansika's baby shower had happened. In that too, Akash remembered Neha's baby shower in his original time. His eyes were welled but there was no one to whom he could say his words. Even his childhood friends had attended his function just like formal guests, as they were too hurt because of his past actions.

Then, it was ninth month. Hansika had come to know that Neha had delivered a baby boy. So, Akash and Hansika had planned to meet her. But as soon as they reached Neha's place, Akash again remembered his days in his original time when he was with Neha.

Then, it was Tamanna who opened the door. Akash and Hansika greeted her and so, she and let them in. Akash knew Neha's parents very well, much better than his present in-laws. As they entered the house, Akash felt as if it is his own house. They had their seats in the living room.

After sometime, Tamanna brought the baby in the living room. "Hey." Hansika said as she saw the child. She wanted to take the child in her hands but she couldn't. So, Akash took the baby with him. But as soon as Akash saw the baby, he was terribly shaken from within. He realised that it was Baadal. He was left speechless. He felt that as if his heart had stopped beating. It was his own child in his hands, but still it wasn't his. He felt that the world had ended for him. He wanted to cry for his baby, but he had to kill the tears inside his eyes. Then, Neha came out to meet them.

"Hey, hi." Hansika said as she hugged Neha. "Congratulations."

"Thank you." Neha replied happily. "What's your update?"

"Waiting." Then, Hansika removed the gift for the child from her bag. "This is for the child."

"Thank you so much." Neha said.

"By the way, what's his name?" Hansika asked.

"Baadal." Neha replied. But, Akash's ears fell numb. He couldn't believe what was all going on around. The child was his own son 'Baadal'. He wanted to take Baadal as his own son, but he knew he couldn't.

Akash had realised that he had lost everything which was his own – his parents, old friends, Neha, and his child Baadal for his time rewind. He had realised that asking for the time rewind was the greatest mistake. He had everything what he had wished for – success, fame, publicity, money, and Hansika. But still he felt like he had nothing. He wanted to go back in his original time.

Then, after some days, Hansika too had delivered a baby. Akash knew that he wouldn't have Baadal as his own child, but still, he was happy for his own child. Then, after a few hours, the doctor came out of the operation theatre and said, "Congratulations, it's a girl." Everyone got excited about hearing the news. "But there is a bad news." The doctor added. Everyone felt silent.

"What's the matter, doctor?" Akash asked nervously.

"The baby has cleft lips and its weight is too low – just one and a half kilogram. And it may not live for long as it is having sudden infant death syndromes." The doctor said. Everyone was startled. Even Akash had got a setback. He wasn't expecting that. He immediately went inside to meet Hansika and the baby. Hansika was crying. "What has happened to our child, Akash?"

"It's because of your drinking and smoking?" Akash said.

"Is it curable?" Hansika asked.

"The doctor says that our baby may not live for long. It's having sudden infant death syndromes." Akash said. Then, even Pratima, Prashant and Tejas entered the room. But as they didn't want to disturb Hansika, they didn't utter a word regarding her habits.

Soon, Hansika was back home. The home welcoming of the baby was done with all the rituals. After the function, when Hansika and Akash were inside their bedroom,

Hansika said, "Akash, I don't want this child. Can we just send her to some orphanage?"

"Have you lost your mind? It's our child. Whatever she is going through, it's all our fault and not hers. Just imagine the pain she is suffering. She needs us. If we won't bring her up then who will?" Akash snapped. But suddenly Pratima happened to visit their room.

"Akash, don't be emotional. This child is going to be a headache for us." Hansika said. Pratima understood what she meant. So, she immediately moved towards her and gave a tight slap on her face. Akash got startled.

"Who gave you the right to slap me?" Hansika asked in wrath to Pratima.

"Who gave you the right to abandon this innocent child?" Pratima asked in the same tone. She was staring right into Hansika's eyes. "We were warning you about your habits. Whatever is happening to this child is all because of you. What kind of mother are you?" Pratima paused for a couple of seconds and again continued, "If you can't handle this child, then give it to me. You have already spoiled my son's life. I am not allowing you to spoil this child's life." Pratima took the baby from Hansika's hand and started walking out.

It was evening when Akash had returned from his studio. Neither Pratima nor Prashant was talking to him and Hansika after the morning incident. After the dinner, he had straight away went to the terrace to spend sometime with himself.

Akash was deeply hurt. He had not wished for that kind of life. That night he was missing Neha and his son Baadal a lot. In his original time, he had a beautiful family, supportive wife, a cute child, and encouraging friends. But due to his time rewind, he had lost everything. He was going on crying. He was crying harder. He didn't want that time rewind. He wanted his original time back. So, he again prayed to God and asked for forgiveness. He was praying harder to get back into his original time, he prayed harder to get Neha and Baadal back, and he prayed harder to get back his parents and childhood friends. He wished 'If I could go back to my original time.'

"Akash! Akash!" Akash heard a faint feminine voice when he was in his deep sleep. The morning rays were poking into his eyes. "Akash, wake up." Akash rubbed the sleep from his eyes and saw that Neha was trying to wake him up.

"Oh! Hi." Akash said. He wondered why Neha was waking him up. "Where is Hansika?"

"Hansika!" Neha was startled. "So, early in the morning, you want Hansika!"

"By the way, who is Hansika?" Pratima asked as she and Prashant were standing behind him.

"Obviously, your daughter-in-law." Akash said.

"Ah!" Neha's jaws went wide open. Even Prashant and Pratima were exchanging baffled looks and wondering what Akash was saying.

"Pa-pa. pa-pa." Akash saw a baby boy running towards him. That child was Baadal. Akash was shocked to see Baadal calling him 'papa'.

"So, now Hansika has suddenly become their daughter-in-law!" Neha exclaimed. Then, Akash saw his book in his hand and realised that it had the same cover page which he had in his original time. He also looked around and saw that it was his old house in Dhran.

"Akash, are you okay?" Prashant asked.

"Oh! It was just a dream." Akash said excitedly. His time hadn't rewind at all. It was just his dream. The time rewind which he had experienced was just his dream. He excitedly took Baadal in his hands and started loving him.

"What dream?" Neha asked as she was flummoxed.

"Oh my son." Akash was going on kissing Baadal all over his face. He was filled with joy to get his son, parents, Neha, and childhood friends back.

"I had tried to wake you up at night. But you were fast asleep." Neha said.

"Thanks to God you didn't wake me up. You won't believe what kind of dream I had tonight." Akash said. "I saw that my time had rewind and I was back to the period when my S.S.C. exams had over. Then I take admission in Arts field for becoming an author along with Hansika. Then I marry her, launch my book, and we both become successful world famous authors. But it also spoils my life. I don't have you and Baadal all with me. So, again I pray to God for bringing me back to my original time, and then I wake up." Neha, Pratima, and Prashant were staring at him in such a way that he had done some crime.

"What happened?" Akash asked nervously.

"Hansika!" Prashant was shocked to know that Akash was dreaming about marrying Hansika. He folded his hands and said, "If I am not wrong, Hansika is Neha's friend. So, why were you dreaming about her?" A total silence spread. Akash realised that he shouldn't have revealed everything. Prashant and Pratima were glaring at him in astonishment. He couldn't answer but just look at Neha for some hint of help while Neha was just holding her mouth to control her laughter.

"Get ready, we are getting late for the shop." Prashant said and left followed by Pratima.

"Do you know, what the problem with you is? You are not thinking about solving your problems right now.

Rather, you are just concentrating on how you would have ignored your problems in your past. So, the thought of time rewind just pops up in your mind again and again." Neha said. "Stop thinking about what you could have done years back and think of how you can move forward form now onwards."

"Through my dream, I have come to know many new things by which I can be a successful author." Akash said.

"That's because you already knew it. You can't imagine things in your dreams which you don't know or didn't know. You already knew it because I had told you. So, Mr. Sharma, always listen to your wife." Neha said and went down.

Akash had realised his mistake. He was always wondering – 'If I could rewind the time.' He had realised that it wasn't possible. So, from then onwards, he was looking forward to attend a good coaching class for authors, take some time to study, and re-launch his book on a wider scale.

Book Description

Akash is a middle-class boy who is fed up with his problems. He always wishes for a time rewind so that he can avoid certain mistakes regarding his career. Soon, he realizes that he can be a good author. He marries a girl named Neha, who always supports him and guides him. But still, he is blank about writing and Publishing.

His first book became a huge failure. So, he gets so disturbed that he desperately wishes to God for his time to rewind so that he can write his book since his early days and be a successful author. So, does his time really rewind? If 'Yes', then what impact does it have on him? Is he able to make good use of it?

The answers are in this book.